The Box

Günter Grass

The Box

TALES FROM THE DARKROOM

TRANSLATED FROM THE GERMAN
BY
KRISHNA WINSTON

Harvill *Secker*
LONDON

Published by Harvill Secker 2010

2 4 6 8 10 9 7 5 3 1

Copyright © Günter Grass 2008
© Steidl Verlag, Göttingen 2008
English translation copyright © Krishna Winston 2010

Günter Grass has asserted his right under the Copyright, Designs and Patents Act 1988 to be
identified as the author of this work

First published with the title *Die Box* in 2008
by Steidl Verlag, Göttingen

First published in Great Britain in 2010 by
HARVILL SECKER
Random House
20 Vauxhall Bridge Road
London SW1V 2SA

www.rbooks.co.uk

Addresses for companies within The Random House Group Limited can be found at:
www.randomhouse.co.uk/offices.htm

The Random House Group Limited Reg. No. 954009

A CIP catalogue record for this book is available from the British Library

ISBN 9781846553073

The Random House Group Limited supports The Forest Stewardship
Council (FSC), the leading international forest certification organisation.
All our titles that are printed on Greenpeace approved FSC certified paper carry the
FSC logo. Our paper procurement policy can be found at www.rbooks.co.uk/environment

Printed and bound in Germany by
GGP Media GmbH

In Memory of Maria Rama

Contents

The Box

Leftovers

ONCE UPON A TIME there was a father, who, having grown old in years, called together his sons and daughters — four, five, six, eight in all. For a long time they resisted, but in the end they granted his wish. Now they are seated round a table and all begin to talk at once, all products of their father's whimsy, using words he has put in their mouths, yet obstinate, too, determined not to spare his feelings despite their love for him. They are still batting around the question: Who's going to start?

The first to come along were two-egged twins. For the purposes of this story they will be called Patrick and Georg, nicknamed Pat and Jorsch, though their real names are different. Then a girl arrived to gladden her parents' hearts; she will answer to Lara. These three children enriched our overpopulated world at a time when the Pill was not yet available, before contraception became the norm and families were planned. Not surprisingly, another child arrived to join the others, unbidden, a gift of capricious chance. The name given him is Thaddeus, but all those seated round the table call him Taddel: Quit your clowning, Taddel! Don't trip on your shoelaces, Taddel! Come on, Taddel, let's hear you do your Clueless Rudi number again!

Although grown-up now, with jobs and families of their own, the daughters and sons speak as if bent on regressing, as if they could capture and hold fast the shadowy outlines of the past, as if time could stand still, as if childhood never ended.

From the table, distracted glances can be cast out of the window at the rolling landscape to either side of the Elbe-Trave Canal, lined with poplars, trees that are condemned to be cut down in the near future, having been officially categorized as a non-native species.

In a large pot a hearty stew is steaming, lentils with lamb chops, which the father has set on a low flame to simmer invitingly and seasoned with marjoram. That is how it has always been: father loves to cook for a crowd. Being the provider is what he calls this tendency towards epic generosity. Wielding his ladle equitably, he fills bowl after bowl, each time murmuring one of his sayings, such as Don't forget that the biblical Esau sold his birthright for a mess of lentils. After the meal he will withdraw to his studio, there to plunge back in time, or he may sit on the garden bench with his wife.

Outdoors, spring has come. Indoors, the heat is still on.

Once they have spooned up their lentils, the siblings can choose between bottled beer and cloudy cider. Lara has brought along photos, which she is trying to organize. Something is still missing: Georg, who answers to Jorsch and has professional training in such matters, hooks up the table microphones, because the father insists on having everything recorded. Jorsch asks the others to test the mikes, and finally declares himself satisfied. From now on, the children have the floor.

You start, Pat! You're the eldest.

You showed up a good ten minutes before Jorsch.

Oh, all right, whatever. For a long time it was only us. To my mind, four would've been plenty, especially since no one thought to ask us whether we wanted to be more than two, three, then four. Even when it was just us twins, we took turns feeling that there were too many of us.

And later on, Lara, all you wanted was a puppy; I'm sure you would've been perfectly content to be the last daughter.

Which I was, for years, though at times I did long for a little sister, as well as a puppy. Then one actually came along, as not much was happening between our mother and our father, and—I assume—he needed someone else, as in fact she found someone else.

And because he and the new woman wanted something they could share and decided they could dispense with the Pill, they had you, another girl, named after father's mother, but now you want to chime in as Lena, the name you've picked for yourself.

No, there's no rush. You two go first. I can wait. That's something I've had to learn. I'll get my time in the limelight.

Pat and Jorsch were almost sixteen, I was thirteen, and Taddel was about nine when we had to get used to a little sister.

And to having your mother around, too, who brought more children, two more girls.

But because our father was still restless, he ran out on his new woman, and that left him at a loose end with the book he was working on, and he would crash wherever he could to type away on his Olivetti.

And while he was roaming, another woman presented him with a girl.

Our beloved Nana.

Whom sadly we didn't get to see till later, much later.

The king's youngest daughter . . .

Make fun of me if you will! But instead of my real name, I want the name of that doll whose life my papa once described in a long poem in doggerel that begins . . .

At any rate, you stayed the youngest. And not long after that father finally settled down, with yet another woman. She brought along you two boys, both younger than Taddel. We've decided to call you Jasper and Paul.

Shouldn't you ask them whether they even like those names?

No problem.

Our real names are completely different, of course . . .

. . . as are yours.

You were older than Lena and much older than Nana,

but family-wise you fitted in, so from then on there were eight of us. Take a look at these pictures—I brought them along especially—here we are, either singly or in various groupings, or here—much later—all of us together . . .

. . . getting bigger and bigger. Here I am, and look at Jorsch's hair, short, then long, and in this one he's making faces . . .

. . . or me putting on a show for the camera, looking bored.

Here's Lara nuzzling her guinea pig.

And there's Taddel moping around in front of the house with his shoelaces trailing.

There's Lena, looking sad.

I bet you'd find pictures exactly like these in most family photo albums. Ordinary snapshots.

Maybe so, Taddel. But sadly, a lot of photos that were anything but ordinary disappeared at some point, and it's a real pity, because . . .

For instance, the photos of Lara's dog.

Or all the shots of me sailing through the air between my papa and my mama on the flying swings, which was something I always secretly wished for. Such a treat.

Or the photo with Taddel's guardian angel.

Or the series showing Paulchen on crutches.

The fact is, all the ordinary pictures, as well as the ones that disappeared, were taken by good old Marie, because she was the only one who . . .

Let me be the one to talk about Mariechen. It began like a fairy tale. Once upon a time there was a photographer. Some called her good old Marie, Taddel called her dear old Marie, but I called her Mariechen. She was part of our patchwork family from the very beginning. Marie was always there, first when we lived in the city, then with you out in the country, also in various places where we went for the holidays, because she clung to father like a burr—that's how she was—and possibly . . .

But also to us, because whenever we wished for something . . .

That's what I'm saying. From the start, when we were only two, then three, then four, she took photos of us or snapped us, whenever father said, Snap away, Marie!

And when she was in a lousy mood—and she could be moody—she'd say, That's all I am, your snap-away-Marie!

But it wasn't just us children she'd snap. She took on father's women, one after the other: first our mama, who looks in every picture as if she's about to leap and pirouette, then Lena's mother, who always has a pained expression, then the next one, Nana's mother, who's forever laughing at god only knows what, and then the last of the four women, Jasper's and Paulchen's mother, whose ringlets are often fluttering in the wind . . .

And in whose arms our father finally found peace.

But even if a group portrait with his four strong women was something he wished for—and I have to agree with Jorsch: a picture of him as a pasha surrounded by his harem must have been high on his wish list—Mariechen insisted on taking them on one at a time. Look here: each in her proper place in the sequence.

But when it came to us, she snapped pictures as if we'd

tumbled out of a dice cup. That's why we have all these photos spread out on the table here, which we can arrange and rearrange—hey there, Nana, stop fooling around with the mike.

But father also wants us to remember all the snapshots that have gone missing, the images Mariechen created of us once she disappeared with those rolls of film into her darkroom.

You need to be more precise, Pat: she took photographs with the Leica, and sometimes with the Hasselblad, but the snapshots were all taken with the box. It was the box, nothing but the box, with which she hunted for images father could use to stoke his imagination. And there was something special about that box, even though it was just an old-fashioned box camera, manufactured by Agfa, which also supplied the rolls of Isochrom B².

Whether it was the Hasselblad, the Leica, or the box, she always had a camera dangling round her neck.

They all belonged to my Hans, old Marie would explain to anyone who admired her cameras. More than those he didn't need.

But only Pat and Jorsch remember what her Hans looked like. You, Pat, said he was a stocky guy with a knobby forehead. And you, Jorsch, said he always had a cigarette dangling from his lower lip.

The two of them had their attic studio on the Kurfürstendamm, between Bleibtreustrasse and Uhland. They specialized in studio portraits of actors and long-legged ballerinas. But also fat vice-presidents from Siemens, complete with wives wearing massive rocks round their necks. And then the brats of filthy-rich folks from Dahlem and Zehlendorf. In their expensive gear, they sat at a slight angle to a backdrop, grinning idiotically or trying to look serious.

Marie was responsible for all the technical stuff—setting up special lights and anything else that had to be done: developing the film, making copies and enlargements, retouching photos to eliminate warts, pimples, lines and wrinkles, double chins, freckles, hairs sprouting on noses.

All in black and white.

Colour didn't exist for her Hans.

For him, there were only shades of grey.

We were young in those days, but I can still hear her saying, when she was in the mood, I was the only one who learned all that stuff from the ground up. Even so, my Hans, who was self-taught, was the one who got to shoot all those folks . . . The darkroom was my department. My Hans hadn't a clue.

Sometimes she'd talk about her apprenticeship in Allenstein. She didn't waste words . . .

. . . that's a village in the Masurian part of East Prussia, father explained.

In Polish it's called Olsztyn now.

That's far off in my freezing homeland, Marie always said, way out east. All gone to the dogs.

Father and mother were very chummy with Hans and Mariechen. They used to sit around drinking a lot and laughing loudly, usually till late at night, telling stories from long ago, when they were young.

Hans also took pictures of father and mother, in front of

a white screen. Always with the Hasselblad or the Leica, never with the Agfa Box No. 54, which was also called Box I and was a huge hit when it first came on the market, till Agfa brought out other models, for instance the Agfa Special with a meniscus lens and . . .

When Hans died unexpectedly, he was buried in the Grove Cemetery in Zehlendorf.

I still remember it. They wouldn't let a priest come and speak, but lots of birds were singing.

The sun was shining right in our eyes. Jorsch and I stood on mother's left, and she stood next to Mariechen. Father was the only one who spoke, over the open grave, about his friend Hans, the black-and-white photographer, and how he'd promised to look after Mariechen, and not only financially.

He spoke softly at first, then louder.

And finally father reeled off the names of all the brands of schnapps his friend Hans had enjoyed.

As you can imagine, the men who'd rolled the coffin out of the chapel and then carried it to the grave — there were four of them, I think — where they lowered it on ropes, worked up quite a thirst as father listed every brand of schnapps, pausing after each one.

That must have sounded pretty solemn.

Like an incantation.

We were squirming; there seemed to be no end in sight.

Let's see if I can remember some of them: Pflümli, Himbeergeist, Mirabell, Moselhefe, or something like that.

One was called Zibärtle — that's from the Black Forest, near where I live.

Kirschwasser was another.

It must have been some time after the Wall went up. We twins were just six then, and you were only two, Lara. You wouldn't remember a thing.

And you weren't even conceived, Taddel.

It must have been in the autumn. Mushrooms everywhere. Under the trees in the cemetery. Growing singly and in clumps. In the underbrush. Behind gravestones. Father's always been crazy about mushrooms and prides himself on knowing every variety. On the way back from the funeral he scooped up all the ones he thought edible.

Filled his hat, as I recall.

And made a pouch out of his handkerchief.

At home we had them with scrambled eggs.

As a funeral repast, he's supposed to have said.

At the time of Hans's funeral, we were still living on Karlsbader Strasse, in a semi-ruin, left over after the bombing.

But when Mariechen found herself all alone in that big studio, she didn't know what to do. Not till father talked her round—he is good at that—did she start taking pictures for him, first with the Leica, then with the Hasselblad, and eventually with the box, almost exclusively with the box: particular items and objects, like the shells he brought back from his travels, also broken dolls, bent nails, the bare stone wall of a building, snail shells, spiders in their webs, squashed frogs, even dead pigeons that Jorsch dragged home.

And later on, fish at the outdoor market in Friedenau . . .

Also heads of cabbage sliced in half . . .

She started snapping those pictures for him while we were still living on Karlsbader Strasse.

Right. It began when father had that book about dogs and scarecrows in the works. It was far from being finished, but he eventually made so much money from it that he could buy that clinker-brick house in Friedenau for us.

And then old Marie visited us there on Niedstrasse to snap pictures of all kinds of things for him . . .

. . . and of us kids. As we got bigger, she lined us up in front of her magic wish box. And for me, only for me, when my guinea pig started getting fatter and fatter, she . . .

That was later, Lara. Jorsch and I come first, because we . . .

I can still see her standing in front of the half-ruined building with her shoulders hunched, the box at waist height, her head bent, as if she were peering into the finder.

But she always shot by feel, often looking in a different direction entirely.

And she had this weird haircut. A bob, father called it.

She looked like a young girl with wrinkles, scrawny and flat-chested. And the box, which hung on a strap, and which she used to . . .

Come on, Pat, you need to be more specific. Let's get the facts straight first. The Agfa box came on the market in 1930 but it wasn't the first box camera. Naturally, the Americans had one even before 1900, the Brownie, which Eastman Kodak sold en masse. But Agfa introduced the six-by-nine format that was later picked up by Zeiss-Ikon's Tengor and Eho's so-called People's Camera. The Agfa box was the first camera bought by ordinary Germans, when its slogan Get more out of life with photography . . .

That's what I was about to say. It was that very box, which Mariechen was given by an uncle or aunt when she was still a young thing and had just started, or maybe just finished, her apprenticeship back in Allenstein.

And that Agfa box came with two rolls of Isochrom and a beginner's instruction booklet, all for sixteen reichsmarks—I looked it up.

And that was the same box she used later to snap pictures of you, Taddel, burying Jorsch's Matchbox cars in the sandbox, and then of my guinea pig when she was . . .

But mostly the two of us, doing flips on the horizontal bar behind the house.

She also snapped pictures of our father on the bar, because when friends came over he always wanted to demonstrate that gymnastics-wise he could pull off an upward circle or sometimes even a full circle with the best of them.

But much later, when Mariechen took pictures of me, though sadly that didn't happen often, she was completely unobtrusive. She would stand off to one side, looking somehow lost, skinny as she was. She seemed alone, not mournful, exactly, which theoretically would have been understandable, more like absent. I'm just a leftover, she told me when she came with my papa, my mother, and me to the Franco-German folk festival in Tegel, where we rode the flying swings, soaring through the air. Such a treat.

Exactly, Nana. She said the same thing about her Agfa box, which looked battered, its corners all dented: This is the only thing left over from all the stuff my Hans and I had, and that's why it means so much to me.

When we asked her, What are you left over from? she would always bring up the war.

Not her Hans's experiences in the war, only the things she considered important. My Hans, she told our father, didn't get home often, except when he had leave or was travelling on assignment. He must have seen awful things at the front. In the east, I mean, and everywhere. Indescribable. Oh dear, oh dear, oh dear.

Her studio must have been somewhere else at the time, still on the Kudamm, but more out towards Halensee.

Father got to hear a long story about that, and Pat and I eavesdropped: Towards the end there, we were bombed out. A good thing my Hans was off at the front and had the Leica and the Hasselblad with him. Not a thing left. The whole kit and caboodle burned to a crisp, while down in the cellar I . . .

Our entire collection of negatives just melted. Nothing left of the lights but scrap. Only the box survived, who knows why. Just singed a bit, especially the leather case it came in.

And then she added, My box takes pictures of things that aren't there. And it sees things that weren't there. Or shows things you'd never in your wildest dreams imagine. It's all-seeing, my box. Must be a result of the fire. It's acted crazy ever since.

Sometimes she'd say, That's how it is, children, when you're left over. You hang around with some screws loose.

We never knew just who or what had screws loose. She or the box, or both.

As for the Hasselblad and the Leica, father told me what happened to them—he'd heard the story several times: My Hans managed to get them through the war. Even though he was a soldier, he never had to fire a gun, just took pictures at the front. That's what he came back with. He also had unused rolls of film, a whole knapsack full. Those were our capital after the war. That's how we got started the minute we heard: Peace is here, finally.

In the beginning her Hans photographed only the occupation forces, mostly Amis, also an English colonel.

Then even a French general sought them out. He paid with a bottle of cognac.

And one time three Russkies made their way up the stairs. With vodka, of course.

The Amis brought cigarettes.

And the Tommies gave them tea and corned beef.

And Mariechen told us one time, No, no, children, we never used the box to snap pictures of the occupation soldiers. My Hans used only the Leica, and sometimes the Hasselblad. To him the box was a reminder of before, when the two of us still had fun together. Besides—but you know this—it has some screws loose, the box. Only when my brother—Jorsch, I mean—refused to let the subject drop . . .

Right, I wanted to know what the deal was . . .

. . . and asked, What does that mean, has some screws loose? she promised, One of these days I'll show you boys what happens when you're left over, have screws loose, and see things that aren't there, or aren't there yet. Besides, you two are still too little and too cheeky, and don't believe the things my box spits out when it's having a good day. It has seen things ahead of time, ever since it survived the fire.

When we went with father to visit her, the two would start whispering the minute she emerged from her darkroom.

She'd send us out on the balcony or give us empty film canisters to play with.

The two of them never told us what was going on, just dropped hints, acting all mysterious. Still, we could guess it always had something to do with that long book of father's, with dogs and mechanical scarecrows. When it was finished, the cover had a hand forming a shadow that looked like a dog's head.

But when we asked him about Mariechen's photos, all father said was, You're not old enough to understand. And to mother he said, It's probably because she comes from Masuria. What our Mariechen sees is far more than we ordinary mortals can see.

And it wasn't till then, but before he'd finished typing his *Dog Years,* that you came along, Lara.

On a Sunday, no less.

Now we finally get to hear about the guinea pig . . .

Hold on, Nana, we aren't done yet.

Somehow our little sister wasn't exactly what we'd expected.

Even before she learned to walk, Lara would only smile tentatively, as father put it.

That hasn't changed.

And then, once she was walking, she'd always veer off to one side—right, Jorsch?

Or you trailed along behind us, never raced on ahead.

Whenever father or mother wanted to take you by the hand, when we went for a Sunday stroll from Roseneck to the Grunewald, you'd clasp your hands behind your back.

And you didn't laugh properly till later, when you got a guinea pig, and then only when the guinea pig squeaked.

You could even imitate the squeaking.

I still can. Want to hear?

And because our Lara never smiled for the camera, good old Marie snapped picture after picture of her.

First on Karlsbader Strasse, then in Friedenau, on the swing at the back of the house, or at the table, with her empty dessert plate in front of her . . .

And again and again with her guinea pig.

Then one time you let her play with the neighbours' guinea pigs, and one of them must have been a male, because before we knew it . . .

That was what I'd been longing for. See, when Taddel came along, and turned out to be a little devil, and there I was, stuck between three brothers, and all I heard was Taddel this and Taddel that, because you were so-o-o little and so-o-o darling, and no matter what got broken, it was never your fault—shut up, Taddel, my turn!—well, Mariechen took pity on me, and with that old-fashioned box of hers snapped pictures for me, pictures of my guinea pig as her belly got rounder and rounder. She'd shoot an entire roll, again and again. And I was the only one she showed the pictures to, not the rest of you. Now that made me laugh. But none of you—not you twins, and certainly not you, Taddel—would believe me when I told you what was in those little pictures she conjured up in her darkroom. I'm not kidding: in each one you could plainly make out three adorable newborn guinea pigs. So sweet, nursing from their mother. The box could predict such things—that there'd be exactly three. And when they were born, it actually was a litter of three. One more adorable than the next. No, all equally adorable. But I hid those photos. Now I had four guinea pigs. That was too many, of course, so I had to give two of them away. By then I was secretly wishing for a puppy—because guinea pigs aren't really that interesting. All they do is guinea pig stuff, eating and squeaking, which stops being fun after a while. But the rest of the family were against a puppy. A dog in the city, where it has no room to run free—what good is that? mama said. Our father didn't really mind, but he delivered one of his pronouncements: There are already more than enough dogs in Berlin. Marie was the only one in favour. So one day, when all the others were busy in the house, she took pictures of me under the apple tree, muttering under her breath old-fashioned words like balsam and salve and emollient. Then she whispered, Make a wish, little Lara, wish for something nice! And when she showed me the pictures a few days later—there were eight—each picture had a tousled puppy in it, sitting on my left or my right, jumping on me, begging, licking, offering me its paw, or giving me a kiss. It had a curly little tail and was clearly a mutt, just like Joggi, when I got him a few years later. But this is our little darkroom secret, Marie said, and she kept all the photos, because, as she said, No bugger will ever believe us.

That's not true—we all believed . . .

You, Taddel, were the only one who didn't, in the beginning . . .

You thought we were off our rockers.

So did you, Jasper, at least at first . . .

. . . but then you had to believe it, when that business with you and your pal turned out to be true.

Do you have to bring that up, Paulchen?

But when Lena and I joined the family much later, we never doubted your Mariechen for a moment, because sometimes she could fulfil our secret wishes, just as she did for you—I mean, we both wished we could have our papa all to ourselves, not just now and then.

Okay, okay, but no one has any proof . . .

That's how I see it, too, Jasper. And to this day I don't understand how I could believe all that stuff as a child and be convinced I'd really seen it. But now that my own little daughter has her heart set on a puppy, just as I did, I'd love to have the kind of wishing box good old Marie had, a box that acts totally crazy when everything around it seems infuriatingly rational. But when my Joggi—first in the photos and then in reality . . .

. . . he wasn't exactly pedigreed.

. . . more like your typical mutt.

. . . and ugly as sin . . .

. . . but still a very special little dog. Everyone acknowledged that, even you boys sometimes. When you weren't quarrelling. And then there was you, Taddel. No wonder I got in the habit of whining, squeezed in between you boys. You called me Squeezebox. Supposedly father called me his Little Squeezebox one time, probably when I needed cheering up. But only my Joggi could really cheer me up. He was a smart little dog, and funny, too. It made me laugh when he tilted his head to one side and smiled. He was also perfectly housetrained, and always looked left and right to check whether cars were coming when he was crossing the street. I taught him that, so he'd know what to do in traffic. Joggi obeyed beautifully. Except that sometimes he'd disappear for hours at a time, gallivanting, you boys called it; that was a habit I couldn't train him out of. Not every day, but about twice a week he'd take off. Sometimes on a Sunday. And no one knew where he was till Marie got on his case. We'll figure it out, my little Lara, she would say. And when Joggi came back from one of his outings, tilted his head as if butter wouldn't melt in his mouth, and smiled, she planted herself in front of him and snapped pictures with her box. Usually standing, sometimes kneeling. Click, click, in quick succession. Now I'm going to lock you in the darkroom! she exclaimed whenever she finished a roll. And sure enough, the very next day Marie brought me, and only me, the prints: eight little photos that showed my Joggi trotting along Niedstrasse, disappearing down the Underground steps on Friedrich-Wilhelm-Platz, then sitting quietly on the platform between an old woman and some guy, then jumping into an open carriage, his curly tail waving. There he was, surrounded by total strangers, wagging his tail, offering his paw, letting people pet him, even smiling, I swear. Next you could see him leaving the train at Hansaplatz, running up one staircase and down another, then sitting calmly on the opposite platform, looking to the left till the train to Steglitz came along and he jumped on. In the last photo you could see Joggi back on Niedstrasse. He was in no hurry to get home. He dilly-dallied along fences, sniffed every tree, raised one hind leg. It goes without saying that I didn't show those pictures to anyone, certainly not to you boys. But when our father or mother would ask, Where's your Joggi? Off roaming again? I didn't lie: Joggi likes to travel on the Underground. Recently he changed trains at Zoo station, on his way to Neukölln, no doubt. Maybe he has a crush on a female there. He's been as far out as Tegel, too. He often goes all the way to the Südstern, changing trains along the way, to stroll along Hasenheide, because it's an area with lots of dogs. Who knows what little adventures my Joggi has on his excursions. He's a typical city dog. Last week he was in Kreuzberg, running along the Wall as if he were looking for a hole where he could slip into the East for a while . . . I'm just as curious as you are to know what he's up to. He always finds his way home, though. But no one was willing to believe me, least of all you boys.

We've heard that story before.

Still sounds crazy to me.

Father told me at the time, Anything's possible, considering the shock the box received during the war when it was the only thing left over, the only thing . . .

And when we rode the flying swings together, my papa

would say, Just wait and see, Nana, everything will be fine some day, when we're together.

Our father certainly knows how to spin a tale.

And afterwards you never know what's really true.

Well, let's let Paulchen explain what was going on with the box, and what was totally made up.

When you were in the darkroom with her, you must've witnessed all her tricks.

She told us you were her assistant.

Right up to the end, too.

Here's all I know: whatever Marie caught with her Agfa showed up exactly in the prints. There was no hocus-pocus, however crazy it may have seemed.

That's what I was saying, just like Paulchen: Joggi looked perfectly normal taking the Underground. He'd go pretty far afield, changing trains several times. Only once he got off at a station nearby, at Spichernstrasse, because he wanted to follow a female—a poodle, I think it was. But the poodle had other ideas . . .

And Joggi had more tricks, but enough of that for now. Once the father has crossed out a few words, toning down an expression here, making another more pointed there, further details occur to him in connection with Marie and her box. The way she often stood off to one side with a bleak expression. The way she would stare at something as if she were drilling holes in it. That was why she seemed alone even with other people around. Before she disappeared into her darkroom, you would hear her hissing under her breath:

curt curses, lengthy invocations of her dead Hans, Masurian endearments.

And he sees a rapid succession of images, each one obliterating the one before it, of Marie standing, her feet close together, or snapping her long-ago shots, click, click, from a crouching position: childlike wishes, obsessive anxieties, but also postscripted and prefigured scenes from the parents' marriage.

That is not what the daughters want to discuss, however, or the sons either; they were not allowed to see these things. It would have embarrassed them to view an entire roll of film showing their mother angrily smashing one wine glass after another while their father looked on in dismay; shards of glass behind the party tent, right after the dancing, because even then, just as many years later . . . That was how all-seeing the box was.

No Flash

THIS TIME THE father has staged a gathering that includes only the four firstborn. They have come together on the site of a former military base, now occupied by Greens, whose lifestyle can be characterized as more or less alternative. Here Pat has found a satisfactory refuge, and has made his siblings an offer: I'll cook spaghetti for you, which is fast, with tomato sauce and grated cheese. I have some red wine on hand, or anything else you want to drink. There's not much room here, but whatever.

His two children are with their mother, as they usually are on weekdays; Pat and his wife are separated. Jorsch had the shortest journey to Freiburg because he is working with a film crew nearby, shooting something along the lines of *Black Forest ER*—he is doing the sound. The same goes for Taddel, who is part of the same team as assistant director.

From the labels of the bottles that Pat puts out on the table it is evident that the wine is from the region. Lara has managed to get away from her family for a few days. It's a relief to be without children now and then.

They all praise the spaghetti. The table at which the siblings are seated has a piece of slate set into the middle for children to draw on. After his stint as an organic farmer, Pat completed an apprenticeship as a cabinetmaker, and he sawed, planed, fitted, and glued the table himself. Everyone admires the orderliness of his cosy apartment, which resembles a set of interlocking boxes. He has built a loft for his daughter and little son, and into the smallest box he has squeezed his study, which resembles a private archive. Cheek by jowl on the shelves are the diaries he has been keeping for years, filled with—well, everything that's happened to me. The way I had to change time and again, make a fresh start . . .

Lara smiles tentatively. This time she plans to hold back. The director, steering the action by remote control, cannot help approving. In any case the twins will be intent on moving along the tale of their childhood.

It's not true, Lara, that only you and father got to see the pictures from Marie's crazy box.

Right, big brother. We were in on the secret when we were only four or five, and you'd just been born, Lara.

Sorry, Taddel, we're not up to where you come in yet.

I don't remember much else, or only hazily, as if through a pane of frosted glass, but the pictures are crystal clear, because up in the attic . . .

We were still in the house on Karlsbader Strasse, where the only other tenants lived below us, to the right of the stairs: an old lady with her son, who was something important with the radio—I'm not sure whether it was Radio in the American Sector or Radio Free Berlin. And all the way down, almost in the cellar, was a laundry.

But to the left of the stairs, all the way up to the eaves, the building was in ruins. Two or three burned-out apartments. And under the caved-in roof nothing but charred rafters, with a Keep Out! sign or something along those lines.

In the cellar, where there'd been no fire damage, a cabinetmaker with a limp had set up shop. He must have been friendly, because he used to give me wood shavings that were as long and curly as the hair of the sixty-eighters would be later on, a fashion we ourselves picked up in the seventies, because we also liked . . .

And the cabinetmaker with the limp was always locking horns with the woman from the laundry, who wasn't just cantankerous; she was a witch. Even mother warned us, Watch out for her, children, she has the evil eye.

I still remember that old witch cursing us because you'd found some dead pigeons in the rubble up in the attic and deposited them in front of the door to her laundry. They were half decayed, crawling with maggots.

Picture this—you, too, Lara: she screamed that she was going to run us through the hot mangle, both of us.

But our apartment, which hadn't caught fire in the war, was a lot bigger than the one in Paris, where we lived in only two rooms because father and mother were always short of cash, and had to scrimp and save. But by now father had made some real money with his *Tin Drum* and could buy legs of lamb for us and all the people he invited to dinner, and could take a taxi into town when he ran out of ideas for the dog book he had in the works.

Sometimes he went to the cinema in the afternoon.

I need the distraction, he'd say.

No doubt he had to take a break from his work now and then, to get some distance.

At any rate, we even had a cleaning lady, and she was supposed to keep an eye on us while mother was teaching the children of French occupation officers to perform difficult dance steps and teeter around on their toes.

That I don't remember. But our apartment was nice, with light streaming in . . .

We had five rooms plus a kitchen and a proper bathroom, and a long hallway, where we . . .

And under the roof, in the undamaged half of the building, father had his studio, with stairs leading up to what he called the gallery.

Our part of town had lots of buildings that were half burned out but had people living in them. And if our family went out walking on a Sunday and we came upon a ruin that had once been a fancy villa, with columns and turrets, you'd always say, Jorsch broke it, because whenever we got a new toy—a car, a ship, or a plane—no sooner had it been unwrapped than ping! it was broken.

Well, I always wanted to see how things were put together and how they worked.

Quality control inspector, our mama called you.

At some point Marie's Hans died. Marie was some ten years older than our father, am I right, big brother? Father must have been in his mid-thirties, but already so famous that when we went shopping at the outdoor market people would turn to look at him and whisper.

It took a while for us to get used to that.

Anyway, not long after her Hans died, old Marie came to Karlsbader Strasse with her box, and first snapped pictures of the outside of our building from all angles, and then all the burned-out apartments from the inside.

She did it because father asked her to. When he said, Snap that for me, will you, Marie? she'd snap away.

His special requests: fish skeletons, gnawed bones, that kind of thing.

Right. Later on, when father had given up smoking everything but his pipe, I saw her take pictures of the used matches he left lying around.

She was even fixated on his eraser crumbs, because every crumb contained a secret, she said.

And earlier, Lara, it was the butts of his hand-rolled cigarettes, remember? Every butt was crooked in its own way, and lay there in the ashtray or wherever, with the burned-down matches . . .

She took snapshots of absolutely everything.

Maybe even of his shit, when no one was looking.

It was the same story with our battered building, which was surrounded by trees, fairly tall ones, too, pines, I think.

But Taddel still doesn't want to believe what Jorsch and I saw when the two of us . . .

. . . it was true, though. Whenever Marie snapped a picture of something with the Agfa box, it came out of her darkroom looking totally different.

It was uncanny at first.

Anyway, we didn't tell a soul, not even mother, that we sneaked into father's studio and saw the pictures . . . Not on his drafting table in front of the big window with the view; no, it was up in the gallery, where he had all his notes tacked to the rafters, all kinds of dogs' names scribbled with a felt-tip pen . . .

That was where he'd also pinned the photos from Marie's darkroom, all in a row.

What those prints showed seemed to come from a different roll of film entirely. We knew how the damaged side of the house really looked. To the left of the main staircase the doors to all the apartments were secured with padlocks, but father had persuaded the janitor to lend him the key, and he let us tag along when he had old Marie go through the building and photograph the interior.

Everything that had been in those apartments at one time, all the furniture and stuff, was now nothing but junk. Spider webs everywhere, with nasty-looking spiders lurking in them.

Holes in the ceilings . . .

Water dripping . . .

It was so spooky that Pat was freaked out. Didn't dare to venture further into those dim caverns. Pigeon droppings everywhere.

Blackened wallpaper was peeling off the walls, and you

could see the newspaper people glued to the walls before the new paper was put on.

We couldn't read yet, but father told us what the papers said, about the things going on in the city and elsewhere long before the war, everyone fighting everyone else. Tales of murder and mayhem. And political brawls, as he called them. Look over here, children, he said, these are the cinema schedules. And here's something about which government has been overthrown. And here a big fat headline about the latest assassination of a politician by right-wing goons.

Of course the two of you grasped it right away, smart as you were.

Sure. And father also read to us about how money kept losing value — the Inflation, it was.

You're right, Taddel. We didn't really get it. We were too young.

But later we did understand what inflation was about, much later, if you really want to know.

The very next day father showed us the place on Koenigsallee where a murder described in one of those tattered newspapers happened. Here, he said, this is where those goons gunned down Rathenau in his open car, which regularly slowed for the curve . . .

There was lots more in those newspapers: ads for shoe polish, funny hats, umbrellas, a big ad for Persil washing powder . . .

Father peeled a few pages loose from the wall . . .

. . . even then he was collecting anything from the past . . .

And—picture this, Lara—in the apartment across from ours we found the remains of a piano.

Actually, big brother, it was a real concert grand, like Jasper's and Paul's mother has in her music room today, which she plays only when no one's listening, not even the cleaning woman, and certainly not father.

At any rate, that piano was more than damaged. Its whole body was charred, its legs were crooked, and the varnish was gone. The lid was missing, too. And the few slivers of ivory still on the keys could be lifted off easily.

Which I assume you two did.

You're not kidding, Taddel.

Not for us, though.

For father's collection.

Those were big apartments like ours, with five rooms plus kitchen and bath. But all the windows had been covered with planks or sheets of fibreboard, so the only light came in through the cracks. It was dim everywhere, in some corners pitch-black.

Still, Mariechen photographed everything with her box—a cracked toilet bowl, battered pails, a shard of mirror, bent spoons, fragments of tiles.

Most of the things had melted in the heat or been hauled off after the bombing, if they were still usable . . .

. . . or had been hacked into kindling right after the war because people had nothing left to burn.

You say it was pitch-black? And even so Marie took pictures with her simple box camera?

Well, she just did, Taddel. She didn't even use a flash.

Holding the camera at waist height, or sometimes kneeling down.

Sure, if we'd been a little older, we'd have thought: It's much too dark in here for taking pictures.

The box can't handle it.

What a waste of film.

But when we sneaked into father's studio, while he was downstairs with friends again, drinking wine and schnapps and yapping about politics, no doubt, we saw the photos tacked to the rafters above his work area, along with the scraps of paper with dog names.

Incredible, those images.

At first you couldn't believe what you were seeing: every picture as bright as day.

Nothing blurred.

Every piece of furniture as clear as could be.

But in the pictures the apartments looked all shipshape and inhabited, though there were no people in them.

What do you mean? Those wrecked apartments all intact?

All neat and tidy, Taddel, that's right.

No yucky spider webs, no more pigeon shit. And one of the apartments looked especially cosy.

The grand piano stood in the middle of the room, undamaged. Sheet music was open on the rack, and the keys had all their ivories in place. There was a sofa in the room, which Marie had photographed a few days before when it was falling apart, so you could pull the stuffing out and see the springs. Now it had nice plump pillows on it, round and square. And sitting on that sofa, propped between two pillows, was a doll with black hair and big eyes who looked something like our little sister. Like you, Lara, when you'd just begun to walk.

And in one of the kitchens the table was set for breakfast for four, with butter, cold cuts, cheese, and eggs in egg cups. I can still see it, that was how sharp those pictures were. Every detail. Salt cellar, teaspoons, and so on, even though Marie hadn't used a flash.

And on the stove, which she'd made a point of photographing, a kettle was steaming, as if someone not visible in the picture, the mother, say, was about to make tea or coffee.

All the flats seemed to be occupied. Some had thick carpets, upholstered chairs, a rocking chair, and pictures on the walls of snow-covered peaks.

And clocks everywhere, so you could've seen exactly what time it was.

If we'd been a little older . . .

In one of those rooms, on a low table, stood a model of a castle, with a tower and a drawbridge. And scads of tin or lead soldiers. Mounted and infantry. Positioned as if they were fighting. Some were wounded, with bandaged heads. And on the floor a model train was set up, with the tracks forming a figure eight and a siding just before the railroad station. A passenger train pulled by a steam locomotive was in the station. It looked as if it was about to pull out, while on the siding another locomotive with a couple of carriages was stopped at a signal . . .

It was a Märklin set. I still remember the transformer.

At any rate, children, certainly boys, maybe even twins

like us, could have played with the castle—that would've
been me—and with the train—I assume that would've
been you.

But Marie had rescued only the objects—the toys, the
furniture, a couple of grandfather clocks, a sewing machine . . .

. . . a Singer, no doubt.

That's possible, Taddel; Singer sewing machines were in
almost every household. All over the world. As I was saying, the breakfast table, the doll in the sofa cushions, the
sheet music on the piano, and who knows what else: that
was what she rescued from the past, without a flash. Only
objects, nothing living.

That's not quite true, brother. There was one apartment,
which in reality was all smashed and so dark I wouldn't have
ventured in there alone, but in the pictures it had the windows wide open, sun streaming in through white curtains,
and among the potted plants a large birdcage. In the cage, on
perches at different heights, sat two birds, canaries maybe,
you couldn't tell because Mariechen's pictures were all in
black and white. And in the pantry of another apartment a
long flypaper strip, and because Marie had taken close-ups,
you could see half-alive blowflies stuck to it, their tiny legs
still intact . . . And in another apartment, full of massive
pieces of furniture, a cat, in one picture asleep on an arm-
chair, in another arching its back on the rug, as if it were
about to hiss. In other pictures the cat was sunning itself
among the potted plants. Wait—it was a striped cat. Now I
remember: in one picture it was playing with a ball of yarn,
or am I just imagining that? Because like father, I . . .

The fact is, Pat thinks a cat was prowling around one of the apartments.

At the time we didn't know why father needed those pictures.

It didn't dawn on me till later: he needed the cat because he was working on *Cat and Mouse,* which involves a sunken Polish minesweeper, a few boys and a girl, and a medal for heroism . . .

. . . and he slipped that in while he was grinding out the huge dog book, but for some reason couldn't seem to finish it.

It's a fact that animals always played an important part in his books, including some who could talk.

But when he had Mariechen photograph those apartments, all he said to us was, Some doctors and a judge lived here. I wish I knew what became of them.

At any rate, we didn't realize till later, if at all, that he needed those pictures so he could form a clearer image of the way things were in the past.

That's how our father is: he thinks purely in terms of the past, even now. He can't shake the habit. Keeps having to . . .

Old Marie helped him out with her magic box . . .

See, we believed everything, Lara, just as you did later, all those things that didn't exist but came out of the darkroom as if they had existed.

And every time Mariechen loaded a roll of fresh film into her Kodak box . . .

It was an Agfa. The label was right there in front, under the lens. How often do I have to remind you? First made in 1930. Before that, Zeiss-Ikon's Tengor was the only box camera. Then the Americans got back into the market with the Brownie Junior, but not till much later, after the war. But Zeiss-Ikon won out with an inexpensive box called the Baldur, named after the chieftain of the Hitler Youth, which our father was in, too, running around in shorts. It cost only eight reichsmarks, that Baldur. They sold hundreds of thousands. There was also one they exported to Italy called the Balilla, made specially for the fascist boys. But Marie didn't take those pictures with a magic or miracle box, as Lara says, but with her good old Agfa Box I. I can still see her with it dangling in front of her stomach.

All right, brother, you win.

I'm only trying to get the facts straight.

At any rate, with her box Mariechen could not only look into the past but also see the future. While we were living in the half-bombed-out building, she produced a whole series of pictures showing what would be happening in politics on the Sunday you came into the world, Lara. I can still see mother holding up those pictures, one after another, above her bulging belly, which she sometimes let us put our ears to, and laughing as Mariechen showed her what had come out of her box. I'm telling you, Lara, and you, too, Taddel: it was a huge herd of sheep. A good two hundred of them, slowly making their way from right to left, from east to west, that is. The shepherd in the lead. Marching beside him a ram with magnificent curved horns. Then picture after picture showing the other sheep. Bringing up the rear, the sheepdog. All heading in the same direction. And then, after you'd been born and Jorsch was sent to pick up the Sunday papers for father at the Roseneck news-stand, they carried stories about a shepherd who'd crossed the border near Lübars, bringing five hundred collectively owned sheep from the Soviet occupation zone to the West, and without a shot being fired, just as Mariechen's box camera had foreseen.

Father also read aloud an article that said no one knew what to do with all those sheep who'd fled the Communist camp to get to the capitalist side. Should they all be slaughtered, or what?

That made him laugh, and then, while almost certainly rolling a cigarette, he claimed that a famous writer, an Englishman, would have celebrated his birthday on the twenty-third of April along with our brand-new Lara—if he hadn't been dead as a doornail for hundreds of years.

All right, brother. It's true about the sheep. The business with the poet—I'll let that pass. But a few months later, not long before our birthday, the Wall was built right through the city so no one could make it across any more, and that was something old Marie had not anticipated, box or no box.

And we couldn't understand why people were panicking and why our mother quickly packed our bags and whisked Lara and us away to Switzerland, which is where she's from.

Why did she do that, Taddel? Well, I assume she was frightened. More for us than for herself. War could have broken out again. Not far from where we lived, on Clayallee, the Americans were already there with their tanks and so forth.

At any rate, father stayed behind in the big apartment and, as we found out later, wrote some strongly worded letters against the building of the Wall—he was that furious.

It did no good, the letter-writing.

But let's suppose, just for the fun of it, he'd gone with Mariechen to Checkpoint Charlie, in the American sector, on a certain day and waited patiently, then said, Now! Snap away, Mariechen! she and her box would have caught a sports car with a Rome licence plate, and in the passenger seat . . .

Right, big brother! And driving that car—let's assume it was a two-seater, maybe an Alfa Romeo—was an Italian, a dentist, let's say, called Emilio, who'd come from Rome to Berlin for the express purpose.

And in the passenger seat would have been a young woman—tall and slender—wearing sunglasses and a kerchief over her head that concealed her curly hair.

And this Emilio would have taken his chances, and not feeling scared at all, would've driven the young woman, who was not only young but also blonde, from the East directly to the checkpoint—even if he'd known that the Swedish passport the young woman pulled out was a fake.

And let's assume—it's only an assumption, Taddel—that Mariechen had snapped a picture of them both from a distance, the real Italian and the fake Swede, right after they'd been handed back their passports and arrived in the West after crossing the People's Police checkpoint, and now, when they were closer, had stopped and got out of the sports car, whereupon the young woman took off her sunglasses and removed her kerchief, revealing her long, curly, flaxen hair, which in the passport photo had looked almost black, straight, and much shorter: if all that had taken place, when Mariechen brought the prints to father from the darkroom later, she could have said, Take a good look at this one. She's something special. She'd be just right for you, if worse comes to worst, I mean, if all else fails.

And further assuming—yes, Taddel, just for fun—if father, left alone in that big apartment, because mother whisked us all away to safety, looked at those eight six-by-nine photos and had a premonition about his second wife, like a vision, simply because after the Wall went up good old Marie had been at a certain place on a certain day, because he insisted on it, and had snapped picture after picture, maybe he wouldn't have . . .

Stop it, you two!

You're both crazy.

What's the point of all these ifs and maybes?

Oh, all right, Taddel.

Just speculation.

A little joke.

But the part about the Italian dentist and the escape—that part's true.

Even the two-seater part is true.

We heard it from Jasper and Paulchen, it was their mother who told them how she made it from the East shortly after the Wall went up, with a false passport, a Swedish newspaper, some Swedish pocket change, and an Italian abetting her escape. Later, that same Emilio got her two sisters out . . .

At any rate, our mother brought the three of us back from Switzerland and unpacked the suitcases.

Obviously, Lara, father couldn't have shown those photos of his second wife to anyone, if they'd really come out of the box.

In any case, Mariechen knew him much better than he knew himself.

Maybe so; she snapped those pictures of his cigarette butts when he was at a loss as to how we were going to keep going as a family . . .

But because he puffed those hand-rolled cigarettes from morning till all hours, later, when it all went wrong, I'm sure Mariechen showed him, with the help of her box, how he could worm his way out of the schemozzle. I could use a hot tip like that myself now and then.

But I remember that after mother brought us back from Switzerland, father kept going off to Schöneberg city hall because there was an election under way and he wanted to help out the mayor of Berlin, who was running against old Adenauer.

You'd see posters for the two candidates all over town.

The old chancellor looked like an Indian chief.

But when we went for walks, father would point out only the mayor's posters and say, That's the one I'm backing. Remember that name.

The posters said *Willy*. Adenauer harped on the fact he was born out of wedlock and had also been an emigrant. That was why father kept going to the city hall and editing speeches for Brandt, to make him a stronger candidate.

Not till it was all over and old Adenauer had won did

father get back to working on his *Dog Years* up there under the eaves.

During that time you could see from photos, taken not by old Marie but by her Hans shortly before his death, with the Hasselblad or the Leica, I assume, that he was getting fatter. He put on weight because he'd contracted some lung problem in Paris.

It was TB.

He had to take pills . . .

. . . and drink cream every day, which bulked him up.

Still, the dog book did get finished. It dealt exclusively with the past, which he visualized down to the smallest details . . .

. . . because Mariechen helped him with her box.

And then, because we were bursting out of the apartment on Karlsbader Strasse, he was in a position to buy us the old clinker-brick house in Friedenau.

He got it very cheap because after the Wall was built real estate prices went through the floor. It was a steal, he said later.

But I remember that before we moved into that house, which workmen were fixing up from top to bottom, old Marie took pictures inside and out, because again father wanted to know who'd lived there before the war and during the war, and who'd done what under the eaves where he set up his new studio and painted fat nuns and scarecrows by the large window.

We'll tell you some other time about the adventures of the old clinker house.

But in the snapshots that old Marie made with her Agfa box of the half-ruin on Karlsbader Strasse, Pat and I saw something our little brother won't want to believe: the sons of a doctor, who may have been the medical director of the Charité Hospital, played there with an electric train set.

But at that time there was no cabinetmaker's shop to the left of the cellar, where I later got wood shavings.

And on the right side there was no laundry yet, with a mangle and an old witch whom I tormented with dead pigeons I deposited at her door till she threatened to put Pat and me through the mangle, slowly, like Max and Moritz.

I remember it all clearly, big brother, even though we were so little.

Stop jabbering, you two.

Okay, okay.

And next time—promise—it's Lara's turn.

And then it'll be you, Taddel.

Strange, the father comments to himself, that Pat and Jorsch can dig the mechanical scarecrows and the lists of dog names out of the rubbish heap of their memory but say not a word about the snowmen Marie had photographed for me, after it snowed through the night and the next day, whereupon I did not prevent Tulla, the child of my whimsy, from rolling the first snowman behind the half-ruin between the towering pines—as was later captured in writing—and, to be precise, on the forest side of the Erbsberg. Suddenly a thaw set in, which is why Jenny, once so plump, no longer had to endure as a swaddled insert but was allowed to step out of the thawing mush, resurrected as a delicate dancer, while the second snowman, which nine masked men, following orders, had rolled on the other side of the Erbsberg, and which Mariechen had also photographed at my request, thanks to the thaw revealed Eddy Amsel, transformed from fat to astonishingly skinny. Both characters survived the dog years in altered form.

Ah, well, how could the children know the way this and that ended up on the printed page, if even their father merely pokes around in the gaps and can only guess where the images came from. In those days, all he had to do was whistle and the words came rushing . . . an inexhaustible wellspring . . . the background swarming with activity and the foreground filled with larger-than-life characters.

Mariechen snapped more than could be dealt with or put in the mouths of the children.

Miracle-wise

THIS TIME IT IS only four of the eight children who gather one weekend to bound back to the days of their youth. This time they are meeting at Jorsch's. With his constantly busy wife and their three daughters he now occupies that same clinker house where every year on their birthdays their father used a pencil to mark his, Pat's, their sister Lara's, and little Taddel's height with the date on the wooden frame of the kitchen door; over the years, all the children succeeded in outgrowing their parents. And as they grew, so did the trees that Pat and Jorsch, barely old enough to go to school, had planted behind the house.

The sons and daughters with other mothers also received invitations to the gathering, but Jorsch had queried whether their presence was absolutely essential, with the result that Lena, who was impatient for her turn, and Nana, who, as she said, theoretically would have liked to sit and listen, both declined, with varying degrees of regret. Jasper and Paulchen felt it was perfectly proper that they were still on the waiting list; Jasper had long-standing engagements that would have made it impossible for him to come.

The summer holidays have just begun, and Jorsch's daughters and their mother are on a trip. A postcard has arrived bearing greetings from a palm-dotted island in southern climes. The siblings sit in the kitchen with its view of the shaded rear garden and the firewall at the back, ivy scrambling up its flaking bricks. Pat is late because he had to visit some old friends. Taddel wants to know all about the new tenant who has moved into father's old studio upstairs. Jorsch, who has recently become the sole owner of the clinker house, with the assent of the rest of the family, explains to his siblings how often and precisely where the old crate desperately needs expensive repairs. Lara listens to her brothers. Then she opens the oven to take out the pizza they had ordered earlier and warmed up. Bottles of cold cider come out of the fridge. At first no one seems to be in the mood to take up the father's tales. All that counts for our father is what can be recounted, Taddel moans.

Finally Jorsch brings up the box again, expressing his doubts as to whether, in the days when miracles still happened, the model in question was the No. 54 box camera, known as Box I: It was probably the successor to that one, the Agfa Special No. 64, with a more powerful lens and diamond viewfinders, with which old Marie . . .

It doesn't matter what she snapped with, Pat says. One way or the other, we believed in it.

Before Taddel has a chance to contradict him, the father, as if with a ghostly hand, positions the microphone in front of Lara.

We were all baptized. You boys and me when we still lived on Karlsbader Strasse. Taddel when we'd already moved to Friedenau. When my turn came, you, Pat, supposedly caused a ruckus. You got bored standing around in the church, because it went on and on. That's what I heard, anyway. Our father wanted the baptism thing; even though he was a non-believer, he went on paying his church tax for years. And our mama, who was brought up on Zwingli's doctrine, as was customary in Switzerland, had turned her back on anything connected with church. Nonetheless she was of the opinion, If it must be, then with all the hocus-pocus, by which I mean Catholic. And when the time came for Taddel to be baptized, our father is supposed to have said, The children will have to decide for themselves what they want to do once they think they're adults; you can resign from any club.

I gather he also said, It can't hurt for them to learn at a young age how everything began with the story of the apple and the snake.

By that he must have meant original sin.

But in addition to the story of Adam and Eve, he told us about Cain and Abel.

And who was allowed onto Noah's ark, and who wasn't.

And everything that came later, all the miracles—the

way Jesus could walk on water in his sandals, how he multi-plied the loaves and fishes, and how he told a cripple, Take up thy bed and walk.

He must have brought up the story of Esau's birthright and the mess of pottage hundreds of times, because we twins were always in each other's hair, and he certainly mentioned it whenever he cooked lentil soup, his favourite dish.

Well, it didn't do us any harm to be baptized, did it?

But did it do us any good?

Everything was different with our half-sisters, though. Lena and Nana were never baptized, and grew up heathens. That's why, when Lena was twelve or thirteen, she took it into her head that she wanted to be baptized, and as a Catholic, too, because that was more meaningful; I assume she felt something was missing from her life. The plan was to have it done before a big audience, at the same time as her First Communion. What a fuss was made over her dress. First it was supposed to be as simple as a nightgown, then she wanted something with ruffles so she'd look like a little bride at her first public appearance.

At any rate, the two of us were there, with Taddel and father, for the whole performance. With full audience par-ticipation, too: standing up, sitting down, singing, standing up again . . .

Mieke and Rieke, Lena's other half-sisters, told me you boys sat there obediently with father in a pew and sang loudly.

No way, only father sang, far too loudly and totally off-key.

We were so embarrassed.

A good thing old Marie wasn't there. With her Agfa's special lens she'd certainly have caught the devil himself and then locked him up in her darkroom, so he . . .

Right, father would have said. Snap away, Mariechen, let's see Mr Satan, disguised as an acolyte, whispering a dirty joke into our Lena's left ear when she hasn't been baptized yet but has already assumed a pious expression.

And Lena, who enjoyed off-colour jokes . . .

Too bad I couldn't be there—I don't remember why. Later, much later, long after I'd had children of my own, and Lena was still in acting school and Nana was fifteen and seemed to be unhappily in love—but unwilling to talk to anyone about it—we three girls went to Italy with our father and visited churches in Umbria, as well as museums, of course. And it was obvious to me that Lena was still a believer. At least it looked that way when she crossed herself with holy water, in Assisi or Orvieto or wherever we went. I almost did so myself, but not quite. And I know that when Nana was in Dresden, training to be a midwife and hung up on that egomaniac, she went to Meissen with you, Pat, when you visited her. To see the sights, I suppose. And in the cathedral there, both of you lit candles before an altar . . . That was true, wasn't it?

We did it because father, when he was a soldier at seventeen and was wounded just before the war ended, was given new dressings in the Meissen castle, which had been turned into a sort of field hospital. I'm sure that was the only reason we . . .

If I'd been there, maybe I'd have done the same thing

for father, even though I'm like Jasper and Paulchen and believe in absolutely nothing. Those two grew up just like me, completely normal.

But they must have picked up some religion, because for years their mother played the organ in a Protestant church, purely as a professional, Sunday after Sunday, and knew by heart not only Bach's organ works but also the entire hymnal, though she wasn't pious in the slightest.

And our Mariechen? What did she believe in?

The box, obviously.

That was miracle enough for her.

It was sacred to her.

Right. At one point she told me, My box is like the good Lord: it sees all that was, that is, and that will be. You can't pull the wool over its eyes. It sees through everything.

And she never doubted that her Hans was in heaven.

But Mariechen, unlike us in the beginning, wasn't Catholic.

Still, she had plenty going on magic-wise, though without wafers, wine, incense, and such.

Father said one time, Our Mariechen comes from Masuria and holds with the old Borussian gods — Perkun and Potrimp and Pikoll and their ilk.

Sometimes she mumbled stuff you couldn't understand, as when she inserted a new roll of film. The phrase six-by-nine was always part of it — the picture format — but it sounded like a magic formula.

That's what I meant. My god, that was all so long ago. I still remember my Communion dress, because old Marie snapped pictures of me from all sides with her magic box.

And some of them she must have taken right before the ceremony, because I'm still wearing a wreath, but my dress is already splattered with chocolate sauce, even though I wasn't allowed anywhere near it till after the ceremony, when all the guests were seated at tables, chattering away; there was that rule about taking Communion on an empty stomach and so forth. But as a child I had a terrible sweet tooth, for pudding, cream torte, whatever. Take a look, little Lara, Marie said, my box always knows in advance what you're going to splatter all over yourself. I've no idea what became of those pictures. Only the photos she took with her Leica, perfectly normal photos, are in my album. But all the snapshots she took with her magic box are gone, like the ones of you, Taddel dear, when you were christened. That was in the Friedenau church . . .

There were two nice chaplains we always enjoyed seeing, because both of them . . .

Later they were reassigned, for disciplinary reasons.

Allegedly they leaned too far to the left.

At any rate, one photo showed lots of people standing around Taddel right after the baptism. And your godmother, a woman with lots of tight curls, was holding you as if you were her own. Our little Taddel was making a face you see him make to this day: a hurt-feelings face. Otherwise it looked like an ordinary christening picture, except that above you and your godmother some sort of spirit was hovering: A guardian angel, old Marie whispered when she showed the picture to me, and only to me. Well, it looked a bit like the guardian angel you see in the TV ads for some insurance company. My little Emma always laughs when she sees it flit across the screen just in time to prevent something awful from happening. Except that the spirit hovering over Taddel was dressed like a football player, wearing proper football boots, which looked ridiculous with the outstretched wings. And Taddel — don't make that hurt-feelings face now! — who was crazy about football from the time he was very young, played with a club in Friedenau. Then, when he lived in the village with Jasper and Paulchen, he played for the local team. And much later, when you'd earned a degree in education to make up for the awful time you had in school, poor thing, you continued to play here and there. Now you and your daughter, who's just as football-crazy as you were, are St Pauli fans, always believing in miracles. Despite all that kicking, you've never had a serious injury, so far as I know; that guardian angel from the magic box must have been watching over you.

But I couldn't really believe in it, even when old Marie showed me the prints.

Whether you believed or not, I'm sure it helped that all four of us Niedstrasse children were baptized, though we no longer believe in . . .

Or only a bit . . .

Like father: I remember at some point he was talking to Pat and me about religion, and he said, The only time I'm religious is when I'm sitting in the woods with paper and pencil, admiring what nature has come up with.

That was his way, whether he sat down after shopping at the open-air market in Friedenau and sketched chopped-off cod heads or did drawings of mushrooms we'd picked on a hike through the Grunewald, back in the days when we were still a proper family.

Remember when Taddel had just been christened and mother and father brought us real Indian outfits from America? They took a ship over, because mother was scared to fly, and they hit gale-force winds and almost sank.

I remember those outfits—deerskin, with fringes.

There was a story in the paper about that Italian ocean liner . . .

And you, Lara, wore your Indian outfit the longest . . .

There were even some deaths, because an enormous wave . . .

You looked like Winnetou's daughter, if he'd had a daughter . . .

. . . a gaping hole just under the bridge . . .

It was a luxury liner, the *Michelangelo*, I think . . .

Just imagine, if Mariechen had snapped a picture of the ship with her box before it left port, the funnels, the bridge . . .

At any rate, our family life was still perfectly normal.

Every year we got a new nanny, so mother could have time to herself.

First it was Heidi, then Margarete, then . . .

And our father, when he wasn't travelling, would sit up there under the eaves, happy as a clam, writing something for which he didn't need old Marie this time, because it was all in dialogue.

You want to bet she snapped pictures of him while he was writing?

It was the play in which workers on Stalinallee and raggedy ancient Romans rehearse an uprising at the same time.

He didn't mind at all when Mariechen took pictures while he was writing.

But some people booed when *The Plebeians* was produced onstage.

When the pictures came out of the darkroom, the theatre looked as if it were going up in flames.

He didn't pay much attention to what the nitpicking reviewers wrote.

It wasn't long before he was up there again, working.

Like that man Uwe, our neighbour in number 14. He sat under the eaves and wrote, too.

A beanpole in glasses, he was.

It bothered him no end that my big brother and I had such strong Berlin accents.

He often sat with father on the terrace in front of the house and had one more beer, and then another.

Those two talked and talked.

Father could make him laugh. We never could, no matter what we did.

There was a lot happening in our clinker house, guests all the time, including some crazy characters.

One night, when father was off working on an election campaign, and you'd just been born, Taddel, the front door was set on fire.

Apparently it was right-wing nuts, who'd used rags and petrol in a bottle.

Things got pretty wild after that.

At night we had cops in the house, guarding us. They were nice, in a quiet way.

And then we went to France for the holidays. All of us, with a new nanny, Margarete. She was a minister's daughter, I think, and she blushed whenever someone spoke directly to her.

And father had only to say the word, and old Marie came along.

Maybe she was his girlfriend.

No way. Mother would have noticed.

I hadn't the faintest notion what was going on.

At any rate, in Brittany, and especially on the long, sandy beach where we were staying, there were all these bunkers left over from the war. Some of them had tremendously thick walls. You could crawl into them—if you weren't scared the way I was.

But they stank of piss and shit.

And from one of those bunkers, a huge dome of concrete with gun slits, hanging askew in the dunes, the two of us jumped off again and again. Jorsch, who weighed less than me, jumped further.

That's why father called me Little Feather. And I remember old Marie snapping picture after picture with her Agfa box as we jumped as far as we could into the dunes.

She crouched in a hollow in the sand and aimed up at us.

Those were instant shots that a normal camera, even the Agfa Special with its three settings, would never have captured, but old Marie's box . . .

. . . which happened to be a magic box and had some

screws loose, which was why she could catch us in mid-air . . .

But later, when Marie developed the photos in her dark-room and showed them to father, he ripped them up, be-cause the box—so he told mother—had turned us into very young soldiers with enormous steel helmets on our heads and gas mask cases dangling round our necks.

Those photos supposedly showed us—first you, brother, then me—taking a running start on the roof of the bunker, then jumping as far as we could, because the invasion had begun along that beach, which you could see in the back-ground, with shells exploding and so forth, and because the bunker may have taken a direct hit, or because we were both scared shitless and wanted to get away, take off, make ourselves scarce, beat it back through the dunes, where . . .

You can understand why father wouldn't want to see that kind of thing: you two as seventeen-year-old soldiers in boots, wearing steel helmets, and possibly armed with sub-machine guns . . . He must have looked just like that during the war. He dreamed about it for a long time afterwards, moaned in his sleep . . .

You're going too far, Marie! he shouted. Probably pretty furious, because he ripped up all the photos.

But Mariechen had a response for him: Who knows what the future holds. That kind of thing catches up with you before you know it.

Otherwise our holidays on the beach where the Atlantic Wall used to be were loads of fun. We went swimming and diving. Father cooked all kinds of fish, including live shellfish, and walked along the beach with you, Lara, at low tide.

You remember?

Looking for mussels . . .

And mother practised dance steps. Without music. Just like that.

Margarete looked after you, Taddel, because you were tiny. All I remember is that from the beginning you liked to play with a ball.

You two are talking total nonsense. I mean that stuff about the bunker and the ripped-up photos. A complete fabrication, just like father's . . . The only part that may have some truth to it is the part about me being ball-crazy before I could even walk.

Later you collected pictures of Beckenbauer, Netzer, and god knows who else.

That's true. But the one I modelled myself on wasn't little bowlegged Müller, even though he scored the most goals, but Wolfgang Overath. That story about the guardian angel, though, that's something you came up with, Lara, or maybe someone else did. I'm sure old Marie would have shown me that photo once I'd left Berlin and was playing on the village team. I even persuaded father to play in our club with the older guys when we were missing a forward in a friendly match with the dockers' team. I got him everything he needed—football boots, a strip. He looked totally cool on the field. At first he couldn't trap the ball, but when we put him on the left wing he made a couple of good crosses. He was even applauded because he stuck it out till the second half. But then he was subbed. Later the Wilster newspaper had a big headline: New Left Wing! They meant it in a political sense, of course, because in those days our father was often accused of being a Red. And in the village a few diehards railed against him. But he didn't score, though it may have looked that way in the photo Marie took of him. When our veterans were trailing four to nothing, she posted herself with her box behind the dockers' goal, and from the photo she took you would have sworn he got the consolation goal, heading it into the top left corner, but she must have pulled off some trick in her darkroom. Anyway, the score was four–one when he was subbed. He was limping and couldn't go on. But he was still proud three days later when he showed me the photo of his headed goal. His left knee was badly swollen, because he was out of shape. He lay on the sofa with an ice pack on his knee and moaned, If only I hadn't . . . I did feel rather guilty, because I'd talked him into it. Right, I said, that header of yours was super! even though the referee from Beidenfleth and everyone in the village was sure it was fat old Reimers from the savings bank who'd scored the goal. I'd like to know how old Marie pulled that one off with her weird box. That and my guardian angel. Wouldn't it be nice if it were real? I could use one. But the picture with father's header is still a mystery.

Well, to this day he believes . . .

So do you two, apparently, with all your talk of the wish box, magic box, miracle box! What'll it be next? I have my doubts. Always did. My thinking was: another example of deceptive packaging. But I didn't say a word to her, because I was never completely sure. At one point Mariechen took

pictures of me in my room, with my big Overath poster as
a backdrop. I had my Cologne FC scarf on for the picture-
taking, and when she showed me the pictures, straight from
the darkroom, it looked as though Wolfgang Overath had
climbed out of the poster and was standing right next to me,
putting the scarf round my neck, then shaking my hand.
Too bad those photos have vanished. They were cool. They
must have gone missing when I—well, you know why—left
Berlin and moved in with father and his new wife in the village. I was the eldest then, and must have really irritated
my new brothers, Jasper and Paulchen.

I'm sure it was because everything was so screwed up in
the family, on Niedstrasse . . .

You just hung around, feeling like an extra wheel.

Which was why our little Taddel needed a new family.

That's how it was. Absolutely. But earlier—all of you say
so—everything was normal, but it only seemed that way.
You two, my big brothers, whom I should have looked up to,
were constantly fighting, and no one knew why. And you,
Lara, whined incessantly. Only your mutt could cheer you
up, and he was ugly as sin, but maybe I was a little jealous
of him. At first I refused to believe that Joggi was taking the
Underground back and forth across the city, changing trains.
Our mother was often preoccupied with herself, and father
sat up there under the eaves, hatching out his crazy stories,
or he had to travel to other countries or go campaigning, so
in the beginning, before I was old enough for school, I always pictured him hunting whales, because *Wahl*, the word
for campaign . . .

In the playground at the corner of Handjerystrasse you

told the other children, My father's fighting a whale, with a real harpoon.

Well, none of my friends laughed at me, but at home everyone laughed, even our mother, who was getting her driver's licence around that time, because our father absolutely refused . . .

He still can't, and won't, learn.

Our first car was a Peugeot.

There was a lot going on in the city in those days, when father was away so often campaigning.

You could see it on television: protests all the time, cops in riot gear with water cannons.

I was three or maybe four by then. I've been told I was always asking questions. But no one gave me any real answers. Certainly not you, my big brothers. You had entirely different things on your minds. With Pat, I'm sure it was girls. With Jorsch, it was his technical stuff. And my father was off hunting whales—I couldn't be persuaded otherwise. It didn't help matters, either, that old Marie showed me at least a dozen pictures, saying, I made these just for you, little Taddel, so you'll know what your father's up to. They were a little blurred, she explained, because there were huge waves in the North Atlantic just then. Still, you could make him out clearly on the cutter, the spitting image, with his walrus moustache, though he was wearing a funny wool cap. He looked terrific. He stood in the bow holding an honest-to-goodness harpoon, taking aim—with his left hand to boot—at something you couldn't make out. But in other photos you could see that he'd hurled the harpoon and hit his mark. The line was completely taut because the whale was pulling, and the cutter was slicing through the water. And so on, till in the last photo you could see the whale's hump with the harpoon sticking in it. I would have been willing to bet I saw my father scramble onto the hump to tie the whale, which was not properly dead yet, to the cutter with a rope. An operation by no means free of risk with such big waves. But unfortunately I wasn't allowed to keep any of the photos. They're a secret, Taddel. No one's supposed to know where your father is and what he's up to, said old Marie.

What a bizarre story.

Sounds like *Moby Dick*, which I'm sure we saw on the goggle-box, and maybe you did, too.

Pat and I knew what the election campaign was about, even if we didn't grasp why it was so important to father that he couldn't let it be. Speeches, speeches, always speeches.

That was the second campaign he threw himself into. Four years before, when you'd just been born, Taddel, the campaign was for Brandt, who at the time was still mayor, and about the Social Democrats, and father painted a poster for them, with a rooster crowing EsPeeDee.

Back then old Marie took entirely different pictures with her Agfa Special. As I was saying, it was before the election campaign that we went to France on holiday . . .

But you couldn't tell from looking at the box what it was capable of. It was a simple rectangular object with three eyes in front. One big one in the middle, two small ones above it on the right and left.

Those were the Agfa Special's brilliant finders, and the big one in the middle was the lens . . .

That's what I'm saying. And on top was a little window for framing the picture, but Mariechen never had to look. And on the lower right side was the shutter release and a crank to advance the film.

And three stops and three distance settings.

That's about all there was to it. Nothing else to see. I held my ear to it—Mariechen told me I could. Nothing to be heard. It was simply a magic box, as you called it, Lara. Or a miracle box.

For a long time I thought that was nothing but talk—the notion that the box could see things that never happened.

That's no big deal, Taddel. Nowadays, with everything computerized and impossible things becoming possible virtually . . .

Back then we were wild about the Beatles . . .

. . . and compared to that, the kinds of fantasy and special effects you see on TV nowadays . . .

One time, when father was in London, he brought us the latest album, *Sgt Pepper's Lonely Hearts Club Band*, with Lovely Rita and When I'm Sixty-four . . .

But old Marie's magic box could hardly compete with *Harry Potter*, visually, I mean.

All you wanted to listen to, Lara, was your stupid Heintje: *Mammy dear, get me a pony* . . .

A pony'd be heaven to me.

Or when dinosaurs come to life on the cinema screen . . .

For us it was only the Beatles, until for Pat the Stones became number one, while I remained faithful to the Mop Tops till I was turned on to Jimi Hendrix, and then Frank Zappa . . .

. . . and all done with computer animation . . . flying lizards and such.

At any rate, we grew our hair long. Pat's was curly, mine more straight, but soon longer than Lara's.

Besides, the stuff going on around us—in the city, I mean—was much more interesting. I was hardly ever bored any more, except on a Sunday now and then. We were too young to be there when the Shah of Iran visited Berlin and the pro-Shah demonstrators went after the students with pipes and roof slats. One student was killed, shot by a cop, but on any surface we could find, Jorsch and I spray-painted Make Love, Not War, and wished we could be downtown where all the action was.

And old Marie caught us in the act of wishing and shot pictures that showed us brothers marching down the Kudamm arm in arm with Rudi Dutschke, a Chilean, and a few other types. Sure, because we were against war, obviously.

Certainly against the one in Vietnam.

But the pictures of us right at the head of the procession, yelling Ho-ho-ho or something, aimed at the newspaper publisher Springer, were only wish photos, like Lara's wish photos or the ones old Marie showed me later. There were a few of me sitting in a car I'd assembled myself that could drive normally but could also fly. It looked like the model I'd constructed from bits and pieces, half Land Rover, half helicopter. But the pictures showed my model full-size . . . In all the prints you could see me piloting it high above the roofs of Friedenau, swooping to the left, then to the right. Below my multipurpose-mobile, on the left, you can make out the tower of the Friedenau city hall. The weekly open-air market is set up in front of the building, with the fat fishwife and the loony florist, both of them waving to me. You can also see Niedstrasse with our clinker house . . . What is it, Taddel?

Just a simple question: How did those totally crazy aerial photos come about?

I'll give you a simple answer: in my room — Pat had his own, which was always neat as a pin, because mother had had a partition put up to separate us squabblers, as she called us — in my room I had all kinds of technical junk, and metal toys I'd received for various birthdays, and I'd constructed a car that could fly. When old Marie saw me fooling around with that flying-mobile in my chaos, as father called my workshop, she exclaimed, Make a wish, Jorsch, quick, make a wish, and in an instant she had her Agfa Special at waist height and aimed, and then she stretched out on her back and pointed it in the air, where there was nothing to see, and snapped a whole roll of film. Later, with her box she even smuggled me into a photo of the Beatles, because that was my dearest wish: I'm playing the drums in place of Ringo Starr, dressed in those cool rags.

She was a sly one with that box of hers.

I saw it more as miraculous.

In those days we still believed in miracles.

Maybe because we were all baptized.

That sounds too Catholic for the father's taste. The children were gullible, even Taddel, who always had both eyes wide open . . . Mariechen would snap pictures into the blue, and

another miracle would be checked off. Wishes would be fulfilled, tears dried, and Lara would smile, which she did so
seldom that it was all the more precious.

The father, however, placed his bets on doubt. His response to the never-ending wars, the proliferating inequi-
ties, the Christian hypocrites, was a definitive No. Sometimes
too loud, sometimes not loud enough. Later, doubt took the
form of a person, surviving underground and convinced
that only snails were immune to doubt. Much of what was
printed and accepted as fact actually happened quite differently, heading credulously in the wrong direction. What
appeared to be rock-solid crumbled. Hopes melted as the
climate changed. And love, too, went astray.

Yet everything followed the calendar: one date after another. Only Mariechen had the ability to suspend and re-
verse the natural course of time. Suspicions captured in
snapshots. Longings pursued and pounced on by a box that
had some screws loose but could reveal hidden states of
affairs . . . Which is why the children must never find out
what their father has suppressed. Not a word about guilt
and other unwelcome deliveries. The only thing about
which there should be no doubt is that once upon a time
there were guardian angels, when Mariechen could prove
everything in black and white.

God-awful Mess

ONCE UPON A TIME, there were four, and later eight, children, who now qualify as adults. But what does it mean to be an adult? Regression is permissible.

At this particular moment three of them are sitting together. As soon as Taddel can get away from the nearby film studio where he is shooting—he was the one who invited his siblings to his table—he will join the conversation. Definitely, he said in his last e-mail.

Lena is busy with her role in Kleist's *Schroffenstein Family*. Nana has the night shift at Hamburg's Eppendorf Hospital. Jasper and Paulchen have not been asked yet. The three eldest fast-forward through the things that are happening in their lives, or are about to happen, or are at a standstill. They lapse into Swiss German, their mother's tongue. Pat complains of marital discord; Georg, known in these pages as Jorsch, is determined to get his temporary financial issues under control. Lara is glad she doesn't have to worry, not yet, about her youngest children. All three enjoy teasing one another as they drink tea and nibble on snacks. Jorsch is the only one smoking.

The many, far too many, kitchen clocks on shelves and atop the cupboard testify to Taddel's mania for collecting at Hamburg's flea markets. His wife, who is pregnant and so smiles for no reason, will later bring to the table a pot of goulash, prepared in advance by her husband, and tiptoe out of the room to commune, still smiling, with her computer. Before being put to bed, her little boy stormed through the apartment and along the corridor to the kitchen, asking the kinds of questions four-year-olds ask, questions for which it is hard to come up with suitable answers.

Now the siblings are eating. Intermittently Pat is on his cell phone, taking care of what he describes as long-overdue business. Once they've polished off the goulash, they sit on the balcony, which offers a view of backyards and a school playground, deserted at this time of evening. Yesterday it rained. More rain is forecast. Yet there are few mosquitoes. In pots on the balcony Taddel's herbs are flourishing, tokens of the domesticity he likes to boast of.

The air quivers with things unspoken. Only gradually do the brothers and sister wend their way into the confused tangle of their childhood. Their speech regresses, sometimes animated, sometimes irritable. They insist that their feelings are still hurt. Because his father wants him to, Pat goes first, stressing pre-emptively that he has no desire to start a fight with Jorsch.

Sometimes I was okay, sometimes not so okay. It hasn't changed that much. But what difference does it make? Anyway, at some point Mariechen would say, Oh dear, oh dear, and Such a god-awful mess, whenever she saw us.

As she always did when something was wrong.

She had a nose for that kind of thing.

Well, it was hard not to notice that things were going downhill with us. Slowly at first, but soon there was nothing more to be done.

We're no strangers to such experiences in our own adult lives.

The moment comes when the flame just goes out.

And in school we were constantly messing up.

Even you, Lara. I know I was.

And Taddel was driving the new nanny—what was her name?—to distraction.

But that didn't trouble father one bit. Maybe because at school he'd been no shining light himself, staying back a year and such.

He hated school.

Well, his mind was always elsewhere.

Still is.

You can never be sure whether he's really listening or just pretending.

I think I remember what he had in the works at the time. Something about a dentist, a teacher, two pupils, and a dachshund that was supposed to be set on fire on the Kudamm, right in front of the Kempinski, to protest against the use of napalm in Vietnam.

It also had something to do with father's underbite.

Dysgnathia, it's called.

When the book was finished—the title was *Local Anaesthetic*—and the jacket image showed—maybe him—holding a finger in the flame of a lighter, it caused him no end of grief.

Man, did the critics ever tear into him when the book came out.

I assume the media jackals wanted him to write about the past and not about the present.

And at some point he started to draw snails and more snails, snails racing and snails in two-way traffic, as he called it.

He was behaving as if at home and otherwise things were perfectly normal.

And our mama's thoughts were elsewhere, too. Maybe because a friend of theirs was getting sicker and sicker. He lived way off in Prague with his family and had . . .

Mother was especially fond of him.

Father liked him, too.

We didn't know what was going on. As for me, I was off on a trip of my own, moved to the basement, because down there . . .

All right, Jorsch, go ahead, tell us.

Well, it started when all of a sudden you had a girlfriend. Maxi was her name. And everybody said, She's so adorable, what an adorable girlfriend our Pat has!

She was really attached to you.

Obviously, because the girls all ran after my big brother, but not after me. It galled me. I was having a streak of bad luck. One time I was hit by a car in front of our house — fortunately all I got was a bruise. Once I tore a hole in my shin on a rusty nail. Father's comment was, It heals fast when you're young — once you're through this phase, Jorsch, things'll get better. He was actually right about that. Besides, I had friends, especially the four boys who started a rock band with me when I was barely fifteen. It was called Chippendale. I think old Marie came up with the name. We were allowed to practise in the cellar.

What a racket you made!

Two of the boys played guitar, one of them bass, and one percussion. I handled the sound. We were pretty loud down there, I'll admit. That's why we only practised when father wasn't working up in the attic. Us boys, we were ambitious, some day we wanted to play a stadium. But the fact is, we never got beyond practising. Then one day old Marie showed up while we were hard at work in the basement, and, holding her box in front of her stomach, she snapped a whole series of photos. Once developed, they showed us on what looked like an outdoor stage where the Stones had put on a huge show recently . . .

You mean the one that ended in a brawl . . .

. . . and there was our rock band performing before a crowd of thousands. No question, it was us up there on the stage. Playing our big number. Hard rock. The crowd was wild. When old Marie showed me the prints, I was speechless. With a bit of a grin, she said, I'll get a freebie when the time comes, you promise, Jorsch? I never showed the pictures to the other boys. I'd have been embarrassed, because those four really had something going for them musically, and they'd have been even more disappointed that we never quite got it together. There was no hope for us, no matter how good they were. Though I had a good ear, I wasn't really musical, and you, Lara, were the only one who practised on that old piano we had standing around, right? But I handled the band's sound engineering: amplifiers, sound board, whatever else was needed. So after I finished my apprenticeship in Cologne, I worked first as an electronics technician and then, after an interval as just a regular electrician, installing sockets, I became a sound engineer. I spent years standing around film and TV sets with headphones on, holding a boom pole. That's how I still earn my modest bread, though now as head soundman. And Pat, our firstborn, had a slew of girlfriends, but he couldn't figure out what he wanted. Admit it, big brother! When people asked you, What do you want to be when you grow up? you said, A cloud pusher. Yet old Marie pointed you in a direction that could've brought a very different outcome. That's right. I mean the idea of the button shop.

There's something to what you say about the girls, at least every now and again. That's how I am. Nothing ever lasted very long. Not with Maxi, either, no matter how adorable she was. She lived way out in the Britz housing estate. We were invited out there to Sunday afternoon coffee, to meet the family. Father and mother and me. Maybe you, too, Lara.

Well, maybe you weren't there, it doesn't matter. Father bought flowers for Maxi's mum from a vending machine at the Underground station, which embarrassed me no end. But we had a very nice time in that high-rise. Their apartment had a terrific view of the city. They had a proper cloth on the table and carpets. And wallpaper in several different flowered patterns. Very homey. Not bare like our house. We didn't even have curtains. And I remember how nervous Maxi was. Even so, it wasn't a relationship for the long haul. All she wanted to do was listen to Mireille Mathieu twittering, and soon I found the whole thing boring—maybe Maxi did, too. There were tears and so on.

And we had to comfort her.

She pined after you for a long time, poor thing.

I felt awful, too. Then I got involved with Sonja, who already had a daughter, a little younger than Taddel. Man, what a difference. A real woman. She knew her way around. Even helped me with my schoolwork. And at some point I packed up and moved in with her, but only one street over, on Handjerystrasse. I was sixteen then, and in our brick house nobody knew which way was up any more. It was so bad that Mariechen didn't feel like snapping pictures of us with her wishing box. All she said when she saw us was, Oh dear, oh dear, oh dear.

Or What a god-awful mess.

Because no one knew what was going on.

I didn't get it either, not till later. Father had come back from one of his trips with a young fellow from Siebenbürgen, in Romania. He'd helped him get out, which can't have been easy.

He looked a little like our father in photos, from the days when he was young and skinny as a rail.

So he was living with us, because our parents thought he was very talented. He'll amount to something one day, they kept saying. First he has to get used to the West; he needs support.

Which is why our mother went all out supporting him, but then . . .

Obviously he needed taking care of.

He was an interesting character. He always looked so solemn, almost tragic.

But father was hardly home, only when he wasn't off campaigning for the EsPeeDee.

Then in Prague, where the Russians had moved in with tanks a couple of years earlier, our parents' friend died from a brain tumour, which I assume was hard on both of them, in different ways, though.

Even so, they went to the funeral together.

They were very silent when they came back.

Spoke to each other only when they couldn't help it, about who would do the grocery shopping and such.

It was impossible not to notice, because in the old days they'd always had lots to talk about—books, films, music, paintings, anything to do with the arts. Never bored, not like me.

And they'd laugh and dance like maniacs when friends came.

We had lots of visitors.

That changed.

Everything changed.

Nothing to laugh about any more.

Everyone tiptoed around the house, because our mama and . . .

As I was saying, you couldn't help noticing, even if I wasn't home very often. I suppose I thought: It's none of my business. I started keeping something like a diary. Still do, whether things are going well or not. At the time I was doing all right, with my steady relationship. We were like a little family. One time my girlfriend and her daughter and I needed buttons for something or other, and we went to a haberdashers on Rheinstrasse. Well, you know the story: that shop had everything. Buttons made of horn, plastic, mother-of-pearl, metal, wood. Some were varnished, some covered with cloth. Every colour under the sun, gold, silver, uniform buttons, too. Square and hexagonal ones. Whole drawers full of buttons in little cardboard boxes, one button glued to the front as a sample. We were amazed. And when the old woman who owned the shop saw how impressed we were, she said, You can have the whole lot. I can't do this any more; my legs are shot. What do you say? I'm not asking much. At that my girlfriend asked, almost as a joke, Well, how much? and the old woman said, Only two thousand marks. It really wasn't that much, but where would we have got that kind of money? There was no point bringing it up with mother, so I spoke to father, who'd just come back from a trip. More as a lark, really: Could you spare two thousand? You'll get it back, I promise. I'll admit it was a whole lot of dough. Mariechen was standing next to him, up there in the attic where the two of them were talking, and I simply asked. First they had to put their heads together. After a lot of whispering, Mariechen must have persuaded father . . .

She could do that . . .

He always listened to old Marie.

She listened to him, too.

They were on the same wavelength.

Maybe because they were both from the East.

At any rate, I got the two thousand and gradually cleared out the old woman's shop. All those boxes, with more than ten thousand buttons. I kid you not. Also cartons full of thread, cotton and silk, and zippers, knitting needles, thimbles, all sorts of stuff. I stowed everything neatly — not like you, brother, right? — in the basement on Handjerystrasse. I built special shelves for all the supplies. Then I labelled every little box with the exact number of buttons it contained.

Also the boxes with the other stuff, the spools of thread, that sort of thing?

Right, all of it! One day Mariechen turned up in the basement and with her wishing box . . .

. . . and — sure thing — without a flash, as always . . .

. . . photographed the entire wall of little boxes and cartons — no need for me to say, Snap away, Mariechen! But no one could have guessed what would come out of her darkroom, not even you. Quite a sight! No kidding, me with a vendor's tray. The kind you wear on a strap round your neck, and in it my most beautiful buttons, including some rare ones, all neatly laid out. Chamois buttons, mother-of-pearl buttons, enamelled buttons, silver-plated buttons. There I stood like a street vendor, with the tray at my waist and my long hair, looking absolutely adorable, as Mariechen trilled. Other pictures showed me selling buttons by the dozen or more. To one boutique or another. And as you could clearly see, all for cash. The boutiques' sales clerks looked ecstatic, because my tray displayed buttons you couldn't find anywhere else, and maybe because they also fell for my long locks. At any rate, one picture showed me being kissed by an older lady. When I saw those photos, I thought: Well, why not, Pat? What harm can it do? Something different for a change. And in the basement, where father had set up a workbench with tools to keep us occupied, I made a vendor's tray out of beech, just like the one I was carrying in Mariechen's photos. It came out nice. You were good with your hands, too, brother.

But more with technical things.

As far as that went, my twin and I were totally different from father, who couldn't screw in a light bulb properly. So with my vendor's tray, which was made of natural wood but stained reddish brown, I went up and down the Kudamm and all the side streets, in and out of chic fashion boutiques, and raked in a heap of money in a short time. At sixteen I was old enough to get a vendor's licence. It was no trouble, and that way everything was on the up-and-up. A year later, when father swung by Niedstrasse on one of his rare visits, I was able to count out two thousand marks into his hand. I was proud of myself, and I assume he was proud of his son, too. But true to my old pattern: just when my business was humming along—because I was selling not only the buttons but also the various threads and the zippers—the fun went out of it. I got sick of making dough, sick of the snazzy ladies in those boutiques.

Right, big brother. You shut up shop because you were bored with buttons.

Or bored *of* them, as you said at the time.

Your heart just wasn't in it any more.

At any rate, I sold the whole lot to a friend of yours, including the vendor's tray and all the buttons and other inventory . . .

Right, to Ralf . . .

. . . simply unloaded it.

And that same Ralf, whom we all came to refer to as Buttonralf, has kept that button business going.

He bought new stock, too, and eventually started making buttons himself, out of cow horn. There was no end to your buttons.

And as I've heard from my friend Lilly, Buttonralf makes a decent living off them.

Which is why you two, but also Taddel, and sometimes even father, kept hounding me: Oh, Pat, if only you'd stuck with the buttons.

For a while there you wanted to become a sort of missionary, and later you had your heart set on farming.

You even pulled it off. And one hundred per cent organic, too. On a real farm, with a barn, a cheese-making operation, and a pipeline from the barn to the milk tank, but unfortunately no horses. You were milking more than twenty cows, twice a day for years . . .

Until—sure thing—my big brother got bored with that, too.

Not true! There were other factors: after the Wall came down and unification altered market conditions . . .

And because your Italian wife . . .

But you were really happy with that vendor's tray full of buttons, which good old Marie had conjured up with her magic box.

Poor Lara, things weren't so happy for you after I left for my apprenticeship in Cologne and Pat moved in with his little family on Handjerystrasse, where his girlfriend helped him with maths and other school stuff till he finally graduated.

After which the whole thing came to an end. Actually she booted me out. But what difference does it make? Maybe the relationship didn't last because I was just too young. At some point later on I hitchhiked to Norway, where I knew a girl who shared my tent till I set out alone for Finnmark. But that's another story.

Oh, come on. The only reason you went north was that when father was your age he hitchhiked way down to the south of Europe.

But before I started on that trip that took me almost to the North Pole, Mariechen had me pose for her box wearing my backpack with a tent strapped to it.

And what wishful image resulted? May we guess?

Probably my brother with a blooming young Lapp girl.

No way. I'm not saying. Except: when I got home she pulled out a few photos of me wandering through the Nordic pampas all by my lonesome. With no compass or map. I was lost. Sitting down on a mossy boulder, howling. Even praying: Don't let me die, dear Lord, I'm so young ... At any rate, those photos that had known everything ahead of time showed how despondent I was. I even scribbled something like a will in my diary. Eventually someone turned up, a game warden, I think. He told me how to get back to civilization.

See, brother, prayer does help sometimes.

But nobody helped me. You were all elsewhere. Before he went off for his apprenticeship, Jorsch was always in the basement with his boys, making the racket they called music. And before you took your big trip up north, Pat, you were hanging out with Sonja, who wore long dresses that looked like nightgowns. It's true—all you thought about was buttons and what you called your new family. I mean your bride and her daughter, who also wore granny dresses with all kinds of flounces and bows. What a farce. And Taddel was always somewhere out there—I wonder what's keeping him now? He was supposed to be here ages ago. His friends were mainly caretakers' children who spent most of their time outdoors. Wishing did no good, either, because old Marie didn't come by nearly as often, and when she did, she just muttered, Oh dear, oh dear, oh dear, such a god-awful mess. She knew exactly why things weren't working out for us family-wise. Father and mother were staying together only out of habit, while both wanted something entirely different. She was focused on her young man, who acted all helpless and looked as if the world was about to come to an end, and father visited us only every two weeks, but didn't feel at home under his own roof. He moped around and acted like a stranger even in the kitchen, because he was actually living with another woman and had bought a house out in the country to that end.

He always seemed to buy a house if enough was left over from a new book.

That book was about the election, but also about the Jews who were driven out of his home town.

All four of us turn up in that snail book. You're in there, Lara, looking for goats on a mountain with him, so they can lick salt from his hand and yours.

And there's even a poem about Pat. It sounds sad, or worried, rather.

And about Taddel, who when he was little hung the word unfortunately onto almost every sentence. In the book he remarks, That's my father, unfortunately. Some of his other expressions are in there, too.

When he read parts of the snail book aloud to me before it was finished, the way he combined different eras I found exciting.

He was working on it before the new woman came into his life.

She was soon pregnant by him.

In the beginning everything was what he'd wished for, he told me when I visited him in the country with Joggi. I really liked it there. The new woman had two daughters, both as blonde as their mother. The whole area was flat as a pancake and so low-lying there were dikes everywhere. The fields were criss-crossed by drainage ditches called *Wettern*. And from the main dike you could look out over a river. There was a ferry you could take from Glückstadt to the village. And not far from there, from another dike, you could see where the Stör flowed into the Elbe. And on the banks of the Elbe you could tell whether it was high tide or low tide. Cows everywhere, and an enormous sky. It was all completely new to me. Later, father gave me a horse, which I'd always wanted. How I used to beg him when we were still a proper family in the city: Please, please. I won't mind if it's small. Just a little bigger than Joggi. It can sleep next to my bed. And old Marie comforted me, Make a wish, little Lara, she would say, and then snapped pictures of me with her magic box, because I used to hang around feeling so miserable hemmed in by my three brothers. As she took the pictures, she mumbled sayings in some old language, and when she showed me what she had conjured up in her darkroom, I was mounted on a real horse, riding like a pro.

Okay, okay, Lara. We know that story.

Just like with your Joggi . . .

So what. In the pictures the horse looked exactly like the one father gave me when he went to live out in the country with his new woman and in the beginning seemed happy. He laughed a lot. Apparently he was crazy about the new woman, who was at least half a head taller than him, and usually wore such a solemn expression that our father had to clown around to make her laugh. But it didn't last long, their happiness. He and the new woman fought too much. Especially after she got pregnant. They fought over everything. Even over a dishwasher. Yet both of them had wanted a child, our Lena. Still, constant quarrelling was something father wasn't used to.

Nothing like that with our mother.

Right. I never heard the two of them so much as yell at each other.

At least not when we were around.

When they stopped talking, laughing, and dancing, they simply fell silent, which was just as bad.

Maybe worse than fighting, which can be bad enough.

Maybe in the end there was nothing left for them to fight about.

At any rate, I was glad I had my Joggi and now a horse, though I couldn't ride it that often, only when I visited them in the village. The rest of the time Nacke stood around in a farmer's field and was sad, because the two daughters of father's new woman didn't know how to ride.

Mieke and Rieke, you mean.

It's too bad that once we were all grown up we didn't get to see them much.

Well, with Rieke living in America . . .

With her Japanese husband and their son . . .

And Mieke has two daughters with an Italian . . .

I was thirteen or almost fourteen when I got that horse—I've no idea why we called him Nacke. But around then my behaviour changed drastically. Before I'd always been so serious, as you say. Now I'd giggle without the slightest provocation and do the stupidest things. But Taddel—too bad he's not here yet—found me idiotic with my adolescent exploits. Fortunately I had two girl friends my age. The three of us could be silly together. One of them was Sani, whose father was Ethiopian. The other one—remember?—was Lilly, and her mother was Czech. We're all still friends, though we don't see one another often. At the time we were thick as thieves. And whenever the three of us got together, we laughed. Taddel—what in the world is keeping him?—said we three made him puke. But old Marie fell all over herself when she saw us. I can't believe it, she said, the three Graces! The same thing father said later to Lena, Nana, and me—My three Graces—when he took us on a three-daughter trip to Italy and we came upon pictures of the Graces in museums. And that's how dear Marie had us pose for her box, time and again . . .

In her attic studio?

Wherever.

Usually on the Kudamm, and also in the Tiergarten. But when she showed us the prints that came out of the darkroom, we weren't wearing our grunge sweaters but had different outfits on every time. Sometimes we were wearing towering wigs and hoop skirts, sometimes sober dresses like queens from the Middle Ages. One time we were dressed like nuns in a cloister, another like whores. In one photo all three of us had our hair bobbed like old Marie's and were smoking cigarettes in long holders, just like her when she was in a good mood. And one time, when she snapped pictures of us wearing our baggy sweaters and jeans, what came out of the darkroom was what we'd secretly wished for: we were stark naked, except for stiletto heels, in which we were strolling down the Kudamm surrounded by staring crowds. In one picture we were prancing along in single file, with Sani in the lead; in another we were arm in arm. In still another snapshot, Lilly, who was more athletic than Sani or me, was doing a handstand naked. And she could do cartwheels, too. But no one was clapping.

And that was what the three of you had really wished for?

Please, please, Mariechen, take us doing a striptease?

In our thoughts, yes. But good old Marie showed us those pictures—there were more than eight of them—only for a few seconds, then tore them all up, the Eve-style ones last, because, she said, not a soul should see you this way, prancing along naked. As she tore them up, she laughed: Ah, to be young like you three duckies, so young! But I didn't always have that much fun. For a long time things were pretty grim. I'm not going to talk about it. When I was sixteen I left school. To become a potter. And father said, You've got what it takes. All that was missing was an apprenticeship. There was no such thing in the city . . .

Well, finally, Taddel.

We were beginning to wonder.

The goulash was delicious . . .

. . . none left for you.

I couldn't get away—too much to do. How far along are you?

Just past the first god-awful mess, when Pat had moved out, Jorsch left for his apprenticeship, father was busy with Lena's mother, nothing was going right family-wise, you were hanging around, and I insisted on having my picture taken with my girl friends on the Kudamm, because . . .

I understand. The house felt emptier and emptier. I was the only one left. And no one, not mother, not father, would explain to me why everyone wanted to run away and why everything was so different, so fucked up. Most of the time I hung out with my friend Gottfried, whose family was like a substitute for my own. And as I said, no one would explain to me why nothing was the way it had been before, Pat and Jorsch least of all. The two of you just left home. When I couldn't figure out what was out of whack or broken between my parents, dear old Marie whispered to me, That's love, little Taddel. Love has a mind of its own. There's no cure for it. Love comes, and it goes. When love's gone, it hurts a whole lot. But sometimes love lasts till death. And then she talked about her Hans, only . . .

That's what Mariechen always did when she was feeling down and wasn't in the mood to smoke her hand-rolled cigarettes in the long holder.

And when she talked about her love for her Hans, she would always say, It lasts, that kind of love, even when there's nothing left to love any more.

Confused as I was, I begged her, Take a picture, Mariechen, so I can see what's going to happen with father and mother. Your box knows such things . . . Even though I never wanted to believe that the box could see more than was really there. But she refused. There was absolutely nothing to be done. Not a single photo. Neither of father and his new woman nor of mother and her lover. All I wanted was a couple of snapshots, to show how long love would last, and so on. And whether the two of them, when they'd finally had enough, would get back in the groove and be together the way they'd been before, when they still talked, laughed, and danced, before the god-awful mess . . . But old Marie didn't want to snap pictures. Absolutely not. And even though she did take a few, far off in the country, where father lived part of the time with Lena's mama, or of our mother having breakfast in the kitchen with her lover, with whom I couldn't seem to get along, she never showed me what came out of the darkroom. When I asked, all she said was, Oh dear, oh dear, and That's how it is with love. That was all I could get out of her. I cried a lot in those days. Only when no one else was around. Up in the attic, where all that was left were father's books, his upright desk, his stuff ... None of you noticed, not even you, Lara, that I'd been crying. You and your girl friends were forever giggling like ninnies. And if I wanted to go into town or somewhere with the three of you, you'd say, You're in the way, Taddel, or You're too little to go where we're going. But before old Marie tore up all the porno pictures she'd cooked up of the three of you in the darkroom, I got to see every one, though just for a second.

You did not!

Yes, I did. The three of you ...

Old Marie would never have shown a single one of those photos.

You want to bet? All eight of them, and others, too. You and your girl friends, those sillies, without a stitch on, parading down the Kudamm ...

Shut up, Taddel.

First you come late, then you stir up trouble.

Just one more thing, then I'll shut my trap.

Promise?

Word of honour, absolutely. In one of those photos you were sitting at a table in the Kranzler Café, naked as the day you were born, surrounded by women stuffing themselves with cakes, in proper clothes, of course.

Enough, Taddel.

And you were spooning up ice cream. But I . . .

Switch off the recorder, Jorsch.

. . . just hung around, clueless, and often cried because all I ever heard was, You're in the way, Taddel! That's enough out of you, Taddel! Only old Marie took pity on me, because everything had changed, and whispered to me . . .

Now the father does not know what to do—should he erase what has been written? Come up with something innocuous in its place, something that skirts the sore points? Or let the debate drag on? Or, against his sons' will, hint in asides at the weed that both of them secretly . . . the smell gave them away? All water under the bridge . . . Or what do you say, Pat and Jorsch?

Some of the children objected earlier when references to father's new woman and mother's lover came up. They were unwilling to accept his wording any longer. The daughters and sons baulked at being participants in his tales. Leave us out of it, they exclaimed. But your tales are also mine, he said, the happy ones and the sad ones. God-awful messes are part of life.

And then he had to admit that Mariechen, who was there with her box even when something out of line happened, had left the really awful things, things that could hurt, in her darkroom or had cut up the negatives. Sheer idiocy! she exclaimed. My box turns away and is ashamed, it has that ability . . .

Now the inadequate father hopes the children will feel some compassion. For they cannot sweep aside his life, nor he theirs, pretending that none of it ever happened.

Make a Wish

EVEN AFTER SO MUCH time has passed, the tears refuse to dry. It's painful, Nana says, and smiles. This time Taddel is punctual and apparently has something up his sleeve, as he had hinted earlier. Jasper and Paulchen are expected later, but will want to chime in as soon as their turn comes. And Pat and Jorsch, who have had theirs, have decided, Jorsch says, To shut up for the time being.

But then Pat insists on contributing a small detail, whereupon Jorsch suddenly casts doubt on the lengthy life of the Agfa Special. He suggests that in the year '36, in time for the Olympic Games, Marie might have purchased an Agfa Trolix with a Bakelite housing. This model had just come on the market and was selling like hot cakes for nine marks fifty. But then he cannot recall any of the particular features of this camera, such as the rounded corners: Maybe she did keep on using the Agfa Special.

In the old half-timbered house near Kassel, the beams, the stairs, and the floors creak. But there is no one around to evoke their past. The summer has been rainy. No one wants to talk about that, only about the two chickens out of five that the weasel got recently.

This time they are meeting at Lara's house. Her three older children from her first marriage have left home, trying to be grown-up, and the two little ones are already asleep. Lara's husband wants to keep his nose out of the family's dirty linen, and has retreated to the next room, presumably thinking about his bees. On the counter sit metal-lidded glass jars of rape honey, presents for the visiting siblings.

Before settling down to talk, the group enjoyed deep bowls of hearty stew: beef with green beans and potatoes. Bottles of beer and juice still stand on the table. Nana has said she prefers to listen: After all, I didn't join the rest of you until later. So Lena, who has just reported on her most recent role, mentioning in passing a rather turbulent love affair, acting out scenes and rendering them comical with imagined dialogue, is now urged to let it all hang out at last. Without hesitation she tries out the table mike, says Testing, testing, this is Lena speaking, and plunges in.

It must have been like in the cinema. Unfortunately it was a lousy film, even if the story had its moments, and at times really heated up. No question, it was love, even a great love, which was why neither of them could let the other go. My papa still says it was passionate. But by the time I'd learned to walk, he was gone, unfortunately. That's why I know only what my sisters told me—they have a different papa, who was also gone, unfortunately. Mieke, the sensible one, filled me in. Both of them liked my papa, though he cooked things that Mieke, who usually ate everything, found totally yucky—like chopped pork liver in mustard sauce. But it must have been quite nice living with him in that big house, which he'd bought just for us and which my mama, who was an architect, had had renovated from top to bottom, lovingly and historically correct down to the smallest detail. It would have made a perfect set for interior scenes in a movie, such as Storm's *Rider on a White Horse*. It was called the Overseer's Residence or the Junge House, because when it was built, several hundred years ago, the whole region was under Danish rule, and the Danes had installed a parish overseer, and much later a shipbuilder named Junge had lived there. Eventually only his daughter Alma was left in the house, and in the village they said she still thumped around up in the attic and in the broom cupboard—I heard all this from Mieke. Anyway, my papa sat around in the big room upstairs, scratching his disturbing images onto copper plates. For example, my sister Rieke's broken doll falling out of the slit-open stomach of a fish, with her legs spread wide and a startled expression on her face. Or he wrote and wrote, trying to make headway on his new novel, the one with a talking fish. But he couldn't seem to finish it, because either in him or in my mama or in both of them at once love would suddenly, or at first hesitantly but then violently, grind to a halt or get too powerful and overheat. Too bad.

Such things happen everywhere.

To me, to Lara also, and to you as well.

But such break-ups are always awful when children are involved, aren't they, Lena?

It was hardest on me.

And not on me?

On you, too, Taddel, I'm sure. But these days I tell myself, Let it go. I survived. The rest of you did, too. Let's talk about that old house instead. I think I still remember the floor tiles in the main room, maybe because I learned to crawl on them or took my first steps. They were glazed in yellow and green, and in the area where the parish overseer had had his long, massive table, round which the village elders would gather, the tiles were so worn that only a little of the bright glaze was left. My papa, who always loved old houses, told Mieke and Rieke, The elders would sit round this table smoking their pipes and debating urgent measures that had to be taken, such as raising or repairing the dikes, because the area was always threatened by floods, which drowned many people and animals. And then he told them about the exorbitant tribute the marsh farmers and Elbe fishermen had to pay the Danes in the form of grain, bacon, and salt herring. Unfortunately I don't remember the times you came to visit, Lara, with your little dog. Nor do I have the faintest memory of when my papa bought a horse for Lara, and also partially for us. He bought it from a real gypsy, Mieke and Rieke said, with a handshake, a horse that was three years old. But Mieke, my big sister, didn't want to ride. No way. So when Lara wasn't visiting, the horse just stood in its stall or was out to pasture on a farm, feeling sad. Or do you think horses can't be sad? You see. I didn't learn to ride until much later, long after the great love between my mama and my papa was over and we were living in town. But then, just like you, Lara, I became horse-crazy, as often happens with girls at a certain age, don't ask me why. I suppose that was why I enjoyed spending the holidays on the pony farm, just like Taddel. But you weren't there for the horseback riding, because actually you were terrified of horses; you came along to look after us, the so-called little ones. You certainly had a big mouth.

What if I did?

You were a real slave driver, ordering us around: Listen, everybody. Pay attention to Taddel.

Well, I was responsible for you kids.

We had to obey you to the letter. First thing in the morning, when everyone was half asleep, we had to shout in unison, Good morning, Taddel!

It got you out of bed, didn't it?

Oh, well, those are just memories. But I dimly recall another feature of that old house: I mean the general store right inside the front door, which had a bell that chimed every time the door opened or closed. That store, which regrettably was no longer in business, had a wooden counter. Behind the counter hundreds of drawers were built into the wall, all of them painted a rich golden yellow, with little enamelled plates that told you what the drawers had contained once upon a time: rock candy, semolina, potato flour, hartshorn salt, barley, cinnamon, dried scarlet runner beans, and who knows what else. My sisters often played in there with me, so good old Marie took pictures of Mieke, Rieke, and me with that box of hers, which struck me as somewhat mysterious when I was older. My papa would come to see us every two weeks and usually stayed with us for two weeks, and sometimes Marie would come with him. On her next visit, she'd bring the pictures she'd developed in the meantime. I hear we looked pretty funny, like in a proper fairy tale. As if we'd stepped off the page of an old picture book, in pinafores and long woollen stockings. With bows in our hair and wearing wooden clogs, we little snotnoses lined up in front of the shop counter. And in those pictures an old woman stood behind the counter, her white hair wound up in a bun, with knitting needles sticking out of it. You could see Alma Junge—that's who she was, the one the villagers said was thumping around in the attic and the broom cupboard—selling my sisters, Rieke and Mieke, but also me, tiny as I was, rock candy and immensely long liquorice laces. You could see the three of us sucking those long, looped-up strings. We must have looked adorable. Maybe that's why I'm still crazy about liquorice drops.

Just as I'm nuts about Nutella, because our cleaning lady, when I was feeling miserable . . .

Hush up, Taddel, it's my turn now. But I hear that my mama, who didn't get to see your Mariechen's photos, was very upset when that blabbermouth Rieke told her about them, and burst out, That's not true. Ghost stories, the worst kind of superstition! My mama and your old Marie apparently had a couple of fights because my papa was forever having private chats with her, and she listened only to him. He must have been utterly dependent on his Mariechen and her box for the photos she made exclusively for him, which he allegedly needed for his book. You know the kind: pictures from the Stone Age, the Great Migration of Peoples, the Middle Ages, and so forth, through the centuries and up to his current confusion. With his typical proclivity for male fantasies, he came up with a new woman for each new phase, and for each of them he crafted one of his typical female stories, until eventually he got stuck and simply couldn't finish the book.

But later it turned out to be a best-seller.

And for a while even the reviewers took a break from . . .

Only a few women's libbers sounded off, because . . .

Let Lena tell us why he couldn't finish *The Flounder*.

Well, because between my papa and my mama, no matter how passionately they'd loved each other, the problems and conflicts kept multiplying till their relationship grew extremely stormy. Their love suffered more and more, and so one day my papa took off, with his unfinished manuscript under his arm. He was simply gone, and unfortunately never found his way back to us. I don't know who was more to blame. No, I really don't want to know. Trying to fix blame does no good. But sometimes, Lara, I find myself wondering. Maybe it was just that my mama didn't mind fighting; she found it perfectly natural, whereas my papa couldn't deal with it, at least not in his own home, where he needed peace and quiet and seemed almost addicted to having things harmonious. I feel sorry for both of them, even though I know from experience that love is rarely an eternal flame. In the plays I act in, seemingly lasting relationships are always breaking up. The theatre couldn't live without crises, the so-called battle of the sexes . . .

Our Pat could tell us a thing or two about that, right, Pat?

As could Lara.

No one's disputing that. But what we children . . .

Come on, Lara, it's your turn now.

I don't know where to start, with all the confusion, or god-awful mess, as old Marie called it, when our father began to turn up more and more often and then came back altogether, with his tail between his legs, and our mama certainly didn't jump for joy when all of a sudden he was standing there, saying, Hello, I'm back. Then he started to settle under the eaves again, but not for long. He looked so sad, sitting up there and riffling through his stacks of paper. In the long run it didn't go well, because our mama was living downstairs with her young man, the one our father had helped get out of Eastern Europe, from Romania, and who was now her lover . . . The house was big enough for all of us, because Pat had been off living in the home of the girlfriend with a child for quite a while, and Jorsch was usually down in the cellar, but soon after went off to Cologne, where father had found him an apprenticeship. Taddel and I were the only ones left. But Taddel spent most of his time hanging out with his friends, and ran around with his shoe-laces untied, probably as a form of protest. So that's how it was; life wasn't easy with all of us under one roof, even though father sometimes came out with pronouncements he may have believed in: Don't worry about me. I'll be quiet as a mouse up there. Have to finish something. It won't be long.

A good thing he had something in the works.

Otherwise he might have gone off the deep end.

But he could have gone back to be there for Lena, couldn't he?

No, that was over and done with. Besides, I don't know whether my mama would have put up with that.

Maybe she would have, Lena. One time your mama came to see us, without you, to have a good talk with our mother, woman to woman, as she supposedly said. And picture this: our father did something he hadn't done in a long time. He cooked some fish dish for the two of them and himself, but also for old Marie, who was there as backup for him. See, your mother and mine talked exclusively about him and his problems, agreeing that he was actually quite nice, solicitous, they both said, but unfortunately he had a bad mother complex or the like. Also that something absolutely had to be done—that's how good old Marie summed it up for me later—to put an end to it: his neurotic behaviour and his conflict-averse tendency to run away from problems, and so on. But apparently father dug in his heels. He refused to go where they wanted to send him.

But there was something to it, don't you think?

They must have gone after him with a vengeance, his two strong women . . .

. . . and together.

The poor man!

Oh, I see, now you two are feeling sorry for him.

In the beginning he just listened, but then, so I hear, he exclaimed, You're not going to get me on the couch! and he lit into them, shouting, I'm the only one who makes a living off my mother complex! And when the two women fell silent for a bit or were busy dealing with fish bones, he added, And on my gravestone it will say, Here lies, with his untreated mother complex . . . But actually, Lena, your mother wanted him back with her and you in the country, which is understandable. And our mother would certainly not have minded, because father was in the way, even when he sat quietly up there under the eaves, the more so because she had enough problems with her young man, who purely character-wise wasn't that easy to get along with. At any rate, while the two women were talking about father and his mother complex as if he weren't there, old Marie managed to snap a few pictures, quickly, as she said, from the edge of the table. But any pictures that emerged from her darkroom she didn't show anyone.

You can only guess . . .

You want to bet they showed our father stretched out on a couch, and the psychiatrist sitting on a chair nearby was unmistakably mother's lover?

Right, he was going to school to study something along those lines . . .

. . . and for that reason was trying—in the picture, I mean—to get father to talk about how even as a little boy he'd told his mama all kinds of made-up stories.

The kind he still likes to tell.

Wait a minute, now I remember exactly what our father cooked for your mother and mine: it was a flounder, steamed with fennel. And that book he was having such trouble finishing was named after the fish he'd steamed.

And the book describes a similar situation—I mean,

where two women, and then more and more of them, are talking about one man while they . . .

At any rate, he stayed holed up in the attic, sitting, or sometimes standing, at his desk and typing on his Olivetti, even though mother would say now and then, At last! At last he's looking for an apartment. But my little brother and I pretty much agreed about one thing, though we often bickered: He's no trouble when he stays up there. And I told my mother, If father has to go, I go, too.

That I don't recall. All I know is that things were tense. And at some point Lena's mother moved out of the house in the country with her daughters and back to town. It's true, in those days I always ran around with my shoelaces untied and sometimes tripped over them and fell in the slush on Perelsplatz or wherever. I'd yell, Shit! The situation was enough to make you run away. No one cared what happened to me. The only place I felt halfway at home was at my friend Gottfried's, in the caretaker's apartment round the corner from us. And now and then our cleaning lady would give me a roll spread with Nutella. Old Marie couldn't help me, either. All she did was moan, Oh dear, oh dear. But she never thought to snap a picture of me with her battered old box. Not even my box can handle such a god-awful mess, she said, it's taking a break. And when father wasn't stewing in his own juice upstairs, supposedly he was out looking for a suitable apartment. But he didn't find one; instead, he found a new woman, and later, supposedly at a birthday party, yet another, and she turned out to be the right one for him, finally.

Mariechen must have been happy.

Right, big brother! She'd had an eye out for this kind of woman when the Wall was first built.

And that's why she'd made a point of positioning herself at Checkpoint Charlie with her box when the blonde with the fake Swedish passport . . .

. . . and an Italian helping her to escape . . .

. . . in an Alfa Romeo, no less . . .

You're both totally nuts. Besides, all that was far off in the future. In between, when father happened not to be living with one woman or another, he was allowed to pick you up from your mother now and then for a couple of hours, Lena. You were the sweetest thing, with your bright little mouse eyes. You had a high, squeaky voice and liked to sing or cry. You sat up in father's studio and played with buttons that I'd picked out for you from Pat's button stock, so you'd have something colourful to play with. Meanwhile father scribbled page after page, because he was determined to finish his book at long last. He wasn't into playing with you, Lena.

He never really played with us, either, when we were little.

You can believe that, Lena.

You too, Nana. Or did he play with you?

But he told us about the book that refused to end, that it would be a sort of fairy tale about a fish that could speak and a fisherman's wife who always wanted more, more, more . . .

Right, he had no trouble telling stories . . .

. . . but he was never keen on playing with his children like other fathers.

So what? He just wasn't a play-father.

Anyway, at some point the house was partitioned.

But not until he had Jasper's and Paulchen's mother all to himself, the woman who was the right one for him, as Mariechen had predicted.

Except there was another involvement before that, which we didn't find out about until later, much too late.

Does that really have to be mentioned?

We didn't suspect a thing, honestly, Nana. About our father and your mother, I mean.

Supposedly it started long before the house was partitioned.

Between one woman and the next, there was one in between.

He really had some screws loose, the old man.

You have to try to understand, Taddel, though it's not easy. Both of them, I mean Nana's mother and our father, had worries of their own. So simply on the basis of worries, the two of them got close, then closer and closer.

And I'm supposed to be the product of all that worry?

That's a form of love, too.

Just look at you, Nana. You turned out so well.

Everyone loves you.

Don't cry, now. There, there.

At any rate, because I'd said that if father had to leave, I'd go, too, the house was simply partitioned. He got the smaller section, to the left of the staircase, and his lair up under the eaves. His part included the pantry as a kitchen, and the room below it with its own shower that had once been our parents' bedroom, and below that was his office, where his secretary sat and typed his letters. It was certainly the best solution. But my girl friends both made fun of the arrangement: It's like having the Berlin Wall down the middle of your house—all that's missing is barbed wire!

And a spiral staircase was installed on our side for access to the rooms upstairs.

Probably there was no other way, and theoretically it should have made sense, because after all the turbulence your mother no doubt wanted to live there undisturbed with her young man, whom she loved, after all.

That's how it was. But he sat where my father used to sit in the kitchen when he'd roasted a leg of lamb, studded with garlic and sage. And now he was the one in the passenger seat of our Peugeot, next to mama, who was driving, because just like father, he refused to get a licence.

As a consolation prize, our father also got the garden behind the house, which was now overgrown with weeds.

I still remember looking out of the kitchen window and seeing him digging up the garden all by himself.

It alarmed us to see him out of there dripping with sweat; he'd never done any gardening. Then he had some rich topsoil delivered, which he carted in a wheelbarrow from the front of the house to the back. Your friends, Gottfried and another boy, helped him. And while digging, he came upon all the Matchbox cars you'd stolen from your brothers and buried out back.

And little Lena was supposed to play with the unearthed cars, but you liked playing with Pat's colourful buttons better . . . or alternated between singing and crying.

In the beginning I thought: Now he's really lost it,

because he'd never done anything like gardening. But then I thought, Maybe he's working off his anger, or he's digging because he's happy to have found a woman at last who'll make it possible for him to finish the book. That was the main thing for him, see. And then, when old Marie came by with her wishing box and snapped pictures from all sides of father digging the garden, I thought, Now we'll get to see how things are going to turn out for him in the future, with one woman or the other. But she didn't show us any of the photos. And when I asked about them, all she said was, What are you thinking of, girl? That's going to stay my darkroom secret.

At some point the divorce was final.

But none of us really knew about it, because the two of them handled it in their usual way, without saying anything.

The only people present were lawyers and, of course, Mariechen, who was always there when something special happened involving father.

I didn't hear until later that they divided everything fifty-fifty, quite peaceably.

At least they didn't fight over anything.

Well, the two of them never fought.

Sometimes I thought: If only they'd had a real knock-down-punch-up, smashing crockery and such, maybe they'd still be together.

Except that then the two of us wouldn't exist, Nana and me.

I suppose the divorce had to happen, because father was determined . . .

But then—listen!—when he and his new wife were already living in the country with Jasper and Paulchen, in the same house where he'd lived for a while with Lena's mother and half-sisters, Mieke and Rieke, and where they put on a grand wedding with lots of guests, your mother brought you into this crazy world, Nana.

So old Marie had another reason to mutter about a godawful mess.

And as usual we didn't find out about it until long afterwards, in bits and pieces.

Maybe there are other children somewhere or other . . .

No, I wasn't happy that my papa didn't confess to me till much later that I had a little sister called Nana . . .

. . . in Sicily, say, where he spent time when he was young . . .

Because he wanted to spare my feelings, he said.

. . . and not even Mariechen's box knew anything about it.

It took me a long time to figure out how many children there were besides me. Theoretically it was nice, because otherwise I'd have grown up as an only child and would have felt lonely much more often, but this way . . .

So it wasn't all bad the way our father handled it, right?

Right, what difference does it make? A few more or less.

Now Jasper and Paulchen joined the family.

Hey, you two got here at exactly the right moment. We were just talking about you and the house in the flatlands along the Elbe.

I understand. You can see it that way, and I'm okay with however you interpret the situation. At any rate, when

Taddel joined us in the village, I wasn't the eldest any more.

But they tell me I cried when Taddel said, Your mother's divorced now and can marry my father.

It wasn't only Paulchen who cried at that time; I cried an awful lot, too. I was often so miserable that Mieke and Rieke had to comfort me.

My own situation was much the same, except that now I had a substitute father who didn't come to see my mother regularly, but was always there when I was feeling really sad because Christmas was around the corner, or my birthday, and I wanted to cry, as I do now, but only because I'm hearing that Lena and Paulchen cried in those days and I tear up easily . . .

What did I tell you.

And all because our poor father had to look for such a long time . . .

I don't believe my ears! You're feeling sorry for him again?

You're right, Lena. At the time I was pissed off, at least for a while, though it certainly wasn't boring — what was going on in the family, I mean. But what difference does it make, I asked myself. At least he was always involved with strong women, all four of them, or even five, if you count Mariechen. Much later, when she was thin as a rail, so thin you could blow her away — or, as father said, Mariechen's just a Masurian handful — she showed me a stack of photos with all the women, each one by herself, but all strong, each in her own way. By then I had my organic farm in Lower

Saxony and was politically affiliated with the Greens. Once, when I had a few days off, I paid a brief visit to our dear old Marie in her Berlin studio, where she was living on nothing but boiled potatoes and pickled herring. Her health was poor, but she was glad to see me. Pay attention, Pat, she said, I'm going to show you something that'll make your eyes bug out. She disappeared into her darkroom, and I sat and waited, though I'd intended to be on my way much sooner to visit friends in East Berlin, because over there ... But when she came out of the darkroom, my eyes really did bug out. A whole stack of prints, all six-by-nines, and all showing things father's various women may have wished for. But more likely the pictures showed those women the way he wished them to be, each one strong in a different way. At any rate, the first photos in the stack showed our father and my mother when they were young. They were dancing, but not on an ordinary floor or a meadow or any kind of solid surface; no, they were dancing on fluffy clouds. It looked like a tango or some such old-time dance.

Rock'n'roll, maybe ...

Their favourite music to dance to was the blues ...

... whenever a Dixieland jazz band played ...

These I snapped when they got divorced, Marie explained. Anyone can take wedding pictures, but an amicable-divorce photo like this, looking back to the early days, when everything seemed so easy and both parties were so full of love and tra-la-la that they thought they could fly—that's the kind of thing only my box can pull off. The box remembers everything, even barrettes—look at this one—that fell out while they were dancing. Then Marie screwed up her face, as she always did when she was furious, and said, I didn't show it to them, this dance in the clouds. They were divorced and finished with each other. Well, I'm not so sure father and mother were finished with each other yet. But what difference does it make? Life goes on. The next photos in the pile from Marie's darkroom showed something like scenes from a silent film. Or rather, like a scene from a Western. Father was leaning against the wheel of one of those covered wagons in which the pioneers set out, going west! With a bloody bandage round his head and his mouth open, he looked dead. And next to him, standing ramrod-straight, was a tall blonde woman clutching a rifle to her chest—Lena's mother, with her hair blowing in the wind. She was squinting as if she were scanning the prairie for Indians, maybe Comanches.

No way. That can't be my mama; she scrambles onto the nearest chair if she sees a baby mouse skittering across the floor.

It was her, though, looking like the last man standing. And peeking out nervously from under the canvas were her daughters, Mieke and Rieke, and between them you, little Lena. All three of you had on old-fashioned bonnets, but you were plainly flaxen-haired like your mother, Lena a bit darker, because . . . And in the foreground lay at least five dead Indians. Maybe your mother would have been capable of such a thing, after all. Father could have gone through thick and thin with her, but he didn't want to. And when dear old Marie had straightened the photos and shoved them under the pile, she said, There's that good old German expression for someone you can trust: he could have gone stealing horses with her. But your father had his heart set on buying horses. And that's what he did, too.

Only one, for Lara. I hear you were quite the sight riding Nacke through the village . . .

With little Joggi trotting along behind us.

This you've got to believe—you, too, Nana. The third batch of photos was even crazier. You would have seen our father wearing a sailor's cap and looking like a revolutionary from the olden days. And standing next to him, laughing and with her hair all tousled, your mother. I'm not lying; neither of them looked worried in the slightest. They were laughing, showing all their teeth. Both of them were positioned behind a barricade and apparently found the whole thing hilarious. They had cartridge belts over their shoulders and a machine gun from the First World War, which another picture showed them aiming and apparently firing. And to their left waved a flag, a red one, I assume—the photos Mariechen showed me were black and white. This kind of thing happened here in Berlin when the revolution came, she said. I don't believe it, I responded. No one, not even a strong woman like Nana's mother, would have got our father anywhere near a barricade. He's never shown any interest in revolution. Was always a reformer. At that Marie giggled: But maybe the mother of your little sister Nana wanted such a thing, and your father, too, just a little. As you children know, my box makes wishes come true.

In reality my mother is totally different. You know her,

Pat and Jorsch, and so do you, Lara. All she cares about is books, books written by other people, which she has to edit painstakingly, word for word and sentence for sentence.

Still, Nana, it's not out of the question that at least secretly she may have harboured a wish . . .

Oh, come on. That's the kind of thing only father could have dreamed up.

But the craziest part was what Marie's wishing box had produced in the fourth batch of photos. You could see a real zeppelin, a medium-size one, tethered to an airport's docking tower. And in front of the cabin, which is quite spacious, with many windows, our father and your mother, half a head taller, standing as if posed for a group photo. In front of them are Jasper and Taddel, and you, Paulchen, are crouching in front of the others. But it's not our father who's wearing the captain's cap. Instead, the pilot of the zeppelin is his second wife.

Obviously, because father can't even ride a bicycle, let alone drive a car.

So are we to assume that he managed to persuade your mother to get a licence to pilot midsize dirigibles?

I know she could do it.

Besides, father always loved the idea of not having a fixed place to live but rather a zeppelin, big enough for him and his stuff — the standing desk and such — and also for his family, so he could land wherever he felt like and be independent location-wise, always on the move and never . . .

That's exactly why good old Marie fulfilled his wish: a strong woman at the helm, and he can devote himself to whatever he happens to have in the works . . .

. . . which also gives him pleasure . . .

Your father always likes to be somewhere else and with someone else, she said. I'm the same. Must have got it from him. Tell me, I asked Mariechen when she was about to gather up the pile of photos and take them back to the darkroom, aren't there any photos of you with father? The make-a-wish kind, I mean. After a long pause, she said, That's enough about your father and his women. For me, it was always dream on, darling. I had to be right there, on the spot, whenever he had a special wish. Then I was to disappear into the darkroom. That was it. Tough luck, ducky! As far as your father was concerned, I was always his snapaway-Marie; there was never more to it than that.

I didn't think old Marie was that bitter!

Maybe she was his sweetheart after all, somewhere in between.

Then I went off to East Berlin, to Prenzlauer Berg, because . . .

Who knows what else we don't know . . .

. . . and what other pictures old Marie had to take . . .

. . . to keep our father supplied, purely in terms of his writing . . .

. . . so when people read him, they could never tell how much of it was true . . .

It's possible even we, sitting here and talking, are just figments of his imagination — what do you think?

That is what he is allowed to do, what he does best: dream up things, imagine things, until they become real and cast a shadow. He says, Your father learned this at an early age. And yet we know, dear Lena, that life does not take place only on the stage. Do you remember the time we left the West far behind, when the lilacs were blooming everywhere, because it was May, and travelled farther and farther into the East, and I asked you, before we set out for Polish territory, to remove all the little birds and butterflies from the nests into which you had braided your hair, because too much bizarre adornment might alarm our Kashubian relatives? A pity that old Marie wasn't there when we sat between Uncle Jan and Aunt Luzie on the sofa under the Sacred Heart picture and you refused to eat the pig's head in aspic. I was so proud to see my little daughter assert herself.

But you, Nanette, she managed to capture with her box even when I could not be with you, but in my thoughts was right there, holding your little hand that completely disappeared into mine. Mariechen knew our wishes, after all. That made it possible for me to be near you when you had dropped your house key or your pocket money again. I helped you look; it was a long way between home and school. Cold, I would say, warm, warmer, warmer, hot . . . And sometimes more turned up than had been lost. The pleasure we both took in found objects.

We laughed and cried together. We could have been seen walking through the Tiergarten or holding hands in the zoo as we stood watching the apes. At any rate, I was with you more often than could have been recorded. All the snapshots showing our happy times together. Ah, if only all those six-by-nine pictures still existed, showing the two of us . . .

Looking Back

TODAY ONLY FOUR of the children have gathered, but later, right after St Pauli's home game against Koblenz, Taddel will join them. Lena has stopped by on her way through Hamburg. And Lara, who grew up with twin brothers and has raised twins of her own, thinks it would be nice to have them absent for a change. Pat is cramming for a test, and Jorsch sent word he could not get away because for weeks he has been doing the sound for a detective series. Nana reported that she is busy delivering babies at the hospital in Eppendorf, and it is not her turn, anyway, but she wishes her siblings a less painful evening than their last get-together, when the sole topic was early sorrow.

They are sitting in the eat-in kitchen. Contemporary art

hangs on every available wall. Since the main subject of discussion will be life in the country, Jasper is hosting the gathering. He returned only the previous day from London, where he was involved in precarious negotiations over financing for a film. Paulchen has managed to join them by moving up a planned trip from Madrid, where he lives with his lovely Brazilian wife. Jasper's wife, who identifies herself as a proponent of contemporary art and a professed Mexican, has just returned from putting their two sons to bed. Now she places a spicy dish in the middle of the table: chili made with black beans and ground beef. Assuming a serious expression and intent on resembling Frida Kahlo ever so slightly, she takes in what she sees as this very German gathering and remarks, Don't pass judgment on your father. You should be glad you still have him. Then she turns and leaves the room. The rest of them remain silent, as if waiting for the echo of her words to die away. Only now does Paulchen say to Jasper, You start this time.

Okay. Someone has to go first. So, Paulchen and I called our mother Camilla. I'm the one who supposedly came up with the name, because our mother, who's the daughter of a doctor, after all, always had a healing touch. On the Danish island where we spent our summers she picked all kinds of medicinal herbs, especially chamomile, and hung bunches up to dry. Chamomile was very good for tea or hot compresses. It was more than just a saying: chamomile is good for what ails you. That's why we'd given her that name when we still lived on the outskirts of town, in the Fuchspass dis-

trict, where our father only came by occasionally for breakfast, which was okay because he and Camilla had worked
things out a while ago. But the new man who turned up one
day didn't call our mother Camilla, but used her real name,
and added a diminutive ending.

And later he called her Sweetie or Dearest, which we
found rather embarrassing.

To me he looked like an old man, though he wasn't yet
fifty. Paulchen and I continued to call your father the old
man, even after he suggested that we call him by his first
name. He resembled a walrus with that moustache. But I
didn't call him that to his face, because in fact we thought he
was okay. It wasn't so easy for you, Paulchen, in the beginning, because you had the habit of crawling into bed with
Camilla when you woke up in the middle of the night—you
know you did. But more and more often the old man was
there, the walrus. And then he brought along this older
woman and just said, This is Mariechen. The only explanation he offered was: Mariechen's a very special photographer, because she has an old-fashioned camera, an Agfa box,
which survived bombs, fires, and burst water pipes during
the war, and since then doesn't work quite right, or works
differently: it's all-seeing and takes the most extraordinary
pictures. And then he added, Mariechen snaps pictures for
me of things I need at the moment or things I wish for. I'm
sure she'll do the same for you boys if you have a very special wish.

We called her Marie.

Taddel also called her old Marie.

At any rate, from then on she was our Marie, too.

In the beginning I was scared of that old woman. I had an uneasy feeling about her, as if I sensed that later on, when I got caught up in something quite embarrassing, she and her box would find me out.

So what was this embarrassing thing, Jasper?

Yes, do tell.

I don't like to talk about it. I really don't. But my little brother—right, Paulchen?—thought Marie was okay. He was thrilled when she snapped pictures with her impossible box of him standing by the garden fence or in front of our row house.

And when we moved from the city to the country with Camilla and the old man, it was fine with me when she came to visit and brought her equipment, not only the Agfa box. We took over the big house that Lena was familiar with. It had all kinds of secret hiding places. And an old-fashioned smell. It even had sleeping cupboards, alcoves, from long ago. And in the front, where you came in off the street, there was a general store, also from long ago—I'm sure Lena's already mentioned it. And our mother's new husband—your papa, I mean, Lena—had settled upstairs in the big room with the yellow and green floor tiles, where he was soon busy with his various projects. He cooked all sorts of weird things for us—pigs' feet, rams' kidneys, cows' hearts, and calves' tongues. But it didn't taste so bad, says Jasper. And he also went to Kelting, the fishmonger in the village—who was slightly hunchbacked but the nicest person—and bought not only sprats and all kinds of smoked fish but also eels, still alive and all slimy.

Once the old man got a grip on those eels, which wasn't easy, he'd hack off their heads with one blow and then saw the rest, still jerking and writhing, into finger-length segments.

Not only those segments but also the heads, which he lined up in a row on the chopping board, were still alive and would even jump off the board. I liked to stand there and watch the eel slaughter, and one time, when I poked a pointy eel's mouth, it locked onto the tip of my index finger and held it so tight that I was scared to death and had to tug like crazy to get my finger free. Marie captured the slaughter of the eels, during which they often slithered away from your father, and the business with my finger, not with her Leica or her Hasselblad, which she hardly used, but with her Agfa box, and later, when she came back to visit, she showed me a stack of six-by-nine prints. You know the kinds of things that came out of her darkroom: weird stuff. These particular pictures showed both my hands, sometimes the backs, sometimes the palms, and to the tip of every finger, including the thumb, an eel's head was attached. In a way it looked quite normal, but also completely unreal, like something out of a horror movie. Right, Lara, it was enough to give one bad dreams. And when I told you about the pictures, Jasper, remember? you didn't want to believe me. It must be a photomontage, you said, and gave a complicated explanation involving American animated films. Yet Marie and her box gave you the willies. You were terrified of her.

That's how it was, I guess. I wonder why, though, because actually she was perfectly okay. She showed us how the Leica worked. And she even let you use the Hasselblad.

Little by little she taught me the technical stuff, aperture settings, the proper shutter speed, and so on. Which is why I later became a photographer, going to school in Potsdam and earning the diploma. No doubt it had something to do with our Marie, who let me watch and learn all kinds of things when I was young. And when your father bought the house behind the dike for her, she let me join her in the darkroom, something she never let Jasper or Taddel do. She'd set it up with what she needed—a red light, trays for developer, fixer, and rinse water, and a printing frame. But she never let me use the Agfa box.

That was the camera she used when she made photos specially for the old man—your father, I mean. From every position, but mostly holding the camera at waist height, without looking in the viewfinder.

And there was a whole series of those eels' heads, still alive, which she'd arranged on the cutting board in a rough semicircle, so they were rearing heavenward and gasping for air—exactly eight of them, I still recall.

And then Camilla's husband, your father, whom we were now calling by his first name, took those photos and etched similar images onto his copper plates.

After the images were printed, it looked totally bizarre, as if the eels were growing out of the ground.

He'd slaughtered the eels for Easter, which may explain why he called the picture *Resurrection*.

Then there were the other pictures she had to take for him, usually, as Jasper said, shooting from the waist. Sometimes she also shot weird images from a squatting position, or lying flat on her stomach on the bank of the Elbe.

Picture this: our Paulchen almost always trotted along behind her when she strode along the top of the dike or across
cow pastures to snap pictures of the cows' bulging udders
for the old man. But I couldn't believe it when Paulchen
told me that the photos showed long, fat eels locked onto
every teat, four of them on each udder. For the milk, of
course — what else would they be after, Lena? You don't believe it? Neither did I. But Paulchen swore it was true. And
before long there they were, on the copper plate the old
man was working on — four fat eels clinging to the udder.
The stories he told us, though, were pure fabrications. For
instance, that at night, and only when the moon was full,
the eels would slither out of the Stör river and over the dike,
then snake their way across the meadows to the cows, which
cows then lay down as if they'd been expecting them, so
the eels could attach themselves to their teats and suck and
suck until they were full, then let go, so the next eels, and so
on. You said so, too, Taddel: Complete fabrication! because
you knew the kind of cock-and-bull stories your father told.
That was when you moved in with us in the village because
you couldn't take it in the city any more, right?

Well, the reason was . . .

Oh, we understand why you left.

And I should have been glad, because as siblings Taddel
and I, purely in terms of sibling relations . . . But once you
were gone . . .

I had to find a new family, no question about it. In
Friedenau I felt absolutely superfluous. I was in the way.
That's what I heard all the time. So I turned into a holy
terror. That I was good at. Whenever my father came from

the country to visit and take care of stuff with his secretary, I'd put on a show, but it was the real thing, because I no longer knew which end was up. And I did that every time, till finally he said, Well, all right, if your mother doesn't mind. At first our mother cried a bit, and then she said yes. I assume she liked Camilla. You'll be in good hands with her, that I'm sure of, she said as I was leaving. And I gave away the two parakeets father had given me earlier to cheer me up, gave them to my friend Gottfried. I adjusted pretty fast to that strange old house, which I first got to know when father lived there for two years with Lena's mother and Lena's two half-sisters. Though in the beginning I was still a holy terror. For instance, I shut Jasper's and Paulchen's cat between an inner window and the storm window, where she went into a frenzy. I know. It was totally insane. Honestly, Paulchen! I must have been out of control . . . What do you think?

Well, yes, but actually you were okay.

You just needed time to settle down.

But I did listen to your mother. Soon began calling her Camilla, too, because she had a way about her, not too soft, not too loud. When Camilla said yes, it meant yes, and when she said no, it meant no. From the beginning she forbade me to call people names like spastic, Turkish pig, and even worse, or rather, she gradually broke me of the habit. She made a halfway tolerable person out of me. It wasn't only old Marie who said so, but you, too, Lara, when you came to visit now and then—without Joggi . . .

We had to have him put to sleep. He was old. Didn't have any spark left.

Taking the Underground, for free—not interested any more. Just lay around under the stairs. And when he did want to cross over to the playground at the corner of Handjery, he no longer looked left or right. Finally I had to give in when everyone, even my girl friends, said, You have to have him put to sleep, no two ways about it—he's just suffering and he stopped smiling ages ago. By then I was the only one left at home. I swear, Taddel, I even missed you, because I felt so lonely. Jorsch was off in Cologne and never sent so much as a postcard. He might as well have vanished from the face of the earth. And Pat was all wrapped up in his Sonja. And then you were gone, Taddel, which I did regret a bit, no matter how much you'd got on my nerves. To make things worse, my first real love went sour. He was a lot older, the kind who couldn't keep his hands off young girls. The girl he took up with after me was even younger, I heard. It's not something I like to talk about. Not at all. And once I'd finished secondary school, I'd had it. I was sick of maths and the whole bit. I wanted to become a potter—I had a talent for making things with my hands, mostly animals, but I didn't want to do artistic stuff like father, rather something that was both useful and beautiful. When I couldn't find an apprenticeship in the city, your Camilla came to my rescue. After driving all over Schleswig-Holstein, she finally found me a spot on Dobersdorf Lake, a lovely area, where her sister was living in a cottage on an estate. I signed up for an apprenticeship with a master potter who was very skilled but a miserable person, which didn't become apparent till later. I really don't like to talk about it, Lena, not even now. At any rate, I was looking forward tremendously to that apprenticeship. And with Camilla, who was practical like me, I got along very well. She took care of everything. Earlier she'd been a professional church organist, in spite of having you two boys, and she'd also managed to take courses in something else. Now she did a terrific job of running the household in that big old place, where something was always going on. Lots of company and such. And our Taddel—you must admit it—was utterly transformed. You took on the role of older brother, and always referred to Jasper and Paulchen as My little brothers.

Paul, whom we always called Paulchen or Paule, was on crutches for a long time. It was father who noticed one day when we were out for a walk that Paulchen was limping on his right leg.

As the village doctor discovered, it was a nasty disease of the bone.

It had some strange name.

Which is why he had to go to a specialist in Berlin to be operated on.

It took a long time before I could get off crutches.

And my father, who was much calmer now that he was living out in the country, was able to laugh like in the old days, and finally finished his massive book. He was determined to have old Marie take a picture with her box of the special shoe Paulchen had to wear on his left foot before the operation.

But Camilla wasn't okay with that. She was somewhat superstitious and wouldn't give Marie permission to take a picture of the shoe.

The old woman actually gave in, though she muttered some kind of witch's curse under her breath.

I had to wear that shoe on my good foot. I called it my monster shoe, because it was so clunky. My right leg was in a brace. And the disease I had was named after the doctor who first identified it. Perthes was his name. It was in my hipbone, which was gradually crumbling away, like dirt, as Camilla said, which was why a section had to be cut out, like a slice of cake. It happened while we were still living in town. I spent a long time in the hospital, sharing my room with a Turkish boy, who was very quiet, even though he had a lot of pain, and was really nice. But I didn't complain much either, Camilla said, though lying in bed so long got tiresome. The nurses were quite gruff, but the head of surgery, who took the saw to my leg, was cool. He was famous for fixing up players from the Hertha football club when they injured their knees or other parts. He set my hipbone so it could grow together properly. And it did, but slowly. Except that since the operation, my right leg's been a bit shorter. Once I didn't need crutches, I got a shoe with a slightly thicker sole.

But you were incredibly fast.

You sure could move on those crutches.

I was amazed when I came to visit.

You were faster than we were crossing the cemetery.

Which is why our Mariechen wanted you to pose for her box, again and again . . .

She shot a whole roll, and then another.

Camilla didn't mind, either.

It was only the monster shoe she couldn't . . .

And Taddel, who otherwise didn't believe in such hocus-pocus at all, would yell, before she snapped a picture of you on your crutches, Make a wish, Paulchen! Quick, make a wish!

But I'm the only one she showed those photos to. A dozen or more. You could see me in a huge department store, KDW, I think — or was it the Europa Centre? — running up and down the escalator on my crutches, even going up the down escalator. I looked utterly insane. Leaping over three steps. And at the top and bottom people were clapping because I moved so skilfully on my crutches. Certainly something I hadn't wished for. I even jumped from the down escalator to the up escalator. And in another set of pictures you could see me back in the village running up and down the sloping bank of the Stör dike. I could leap over fences. I even managed a somersault on crutches. But only in those photos.

After that you trotted after her like a puppy whenever she crossed the dike and headed off towards Hollerwettern.

I hobbled all the way to the Elbe dike, where she snapped pictures of ships far off in the distance with her Agfa box, which was meant to be used only for close-ups in good weather. And those pictures she took in foul weather showed huge tankers and freighters loaded with containers, coming from Hamburg or heading towards Hamburg. From that dike she also photographed warships, both domestic and foreign. One time it was an aircraft carrier coming from England for a naval visit. What a sight. I didn't say anything, but I thought to myself, I'd really like to know.

I'm willing to bet she was snapping those pictures for father, because he'd finished that long book and now had something short and sweet in the works, to help him recuperate, he told Camilla.

The story was supposed to take place during the Thirty Years' War, shortly before it ended.

He wanted the box to help him rewind.

In those days the entire Krempe Marsh and also the Wilster Marsh were apparently occupied by the Danes, and in the middle of the war Glückstadt and Krempe came under siege from—I'm not sure, either the Swedes, who had it in for the Danes, or from Wallenstein. The old man knew all kinds of stuff about him, including the fact that in addition to the sieges, a real naval battle took place on the Elbe. That was why those photos our Marie snapped from the Elbe dike of the most modern warships, with nothing but her plain little box and a few tricks, were supposed to bring back to life all the things we'd slogged through in history class.

That's how it was. See, father, who really knew his history, wanted every detail to be, as he told her, as graphic as possible: I want to know how many sails the Swedes have hoisted and how many cannon are mounted on the Danish ships . . .

Historical snapshots is what the old man called that kind of thing. And she delivered, singly and serially . . .

. . . because she did everything father wished for, whatever the weather . . .

Even in the middle of a nor'wester you could see her up

on the Elbe dike. She leaned into the wind, snapping picture after picture. And our Paulchen, on crutches at the time, always by her side.

So? Camilla had no problem with it. At least she never objected when Mariechen supplied the most unbelievable material.

The comment we always heard was, There are some things your imagination can't dream up.

And sometimes Camilla said, Later, when the whole story's been told, you'll be able to read it.

She gave us stacks of books written by other people.

More and more of them.

One I remember was *The Catcher in the Rye*.

But Jasper was the only bookworm. He read everything he could lay his hands on, though nothing by father.

When he was young, Pat read Bravo comics, and only got round to newspapers and novels much later . . .

. . . but Jorsch read almost every word Jules Verne ever wrote . . .

It's true: there were too many books in the house, with the result that education-wise we didn't get interested till later, much later.

Jasper was the only exception.

He read enough for all the rest of us.

Certainly for me. In those days the only thing I cared to read was *Kicker*, which published all the football scores.

But for the new book, which wasn't supposed to turn out as long as the one before, he was still hunting for motifs, as Camilla said . . .

Which was why old Marie was constantly roving through the cemetery.

She snapped pictures of the ancient gravestones around the church.

You want to bet that when she disappeared into her darkroom all the dead people scrambled out of their graves and hopped around, one hundred per cent alive, wearing outfits from bygone times such as knee breeches and wigs?

At any rate, the old man set out for the Münster region with Camilla, Paulchen, and me in our Mercedes station wagon—you didn't want to come along, Taddel . . .

. . . without Marie this time, who maybe didn't feel like it, like Taddel, or was just in a bad mood . . .

But she lent your father the box, something she never did otherwise.

And when we got to Telgte, he snapped pictures with Marie's box of the motifs and such that he still needed.

He, who never took pictures, snapped several rolls.

At that point I didn't need the crutches any more. I showed him how to use the Agfa; obviously he couldn't do it by feel, holding the box at waist height, the way Marie did.

But I saw that all he had in the viewfinder was an ordinary parking lot, almost deserted. The shot would have shown nothing but concrete.

It was an island, that parking lot, because a river curved round it on the right and the left, and where the river came together again stood the ruins of an old mill . . .

He also snapped pictures of what was left of the mill.

But mainly he was intent on capturing the completely

paved-over lot. Because, he said, in this very spot a good three hundred years ago stood the Brückenhof, which will be the scene of the action. It must have been a sort of hostel for travelling merchants who planned to take the bridges over the Ems with their wares, I mean bales of cloth and full kegs.

In those days, your father said, there was a war going on that wouldn't end, though peace talks had been under way for years in Münster and Osnabrück. And all the rooms in the hostel that existed in this spot were at one time occupied by writers, who planned to meet where today there was nothing but the nearly deserted parking lot.

And the writers apparently read aloud from their books. Complicated stuff, baroque poetry and such.

And all this because when Taddel's father was a very young writer himself he attended similar meetings with a bunch of other writers in one location or another.

He must have shot at least three rolls of film in that parking lot. And I helped him put in the rolls and take them out. They have to be positioned on the spool with the red side of the protective strip facing out. He didn't know how to do that. But he caught on fast. The main thing in any case was that the box secretly . . .

There were only a few people in the parking lot who stared, because they'd recognized the old man as he snapped away.

It was awkward.

Maybe father looked familiar and they were wondering what this fellow with the moustache was doing there.

Of course, Lara. They probably thought bodies were buried there that he intended to dig up, one at a time.

But the staring didn't bother him.

It was exciting, though, to hear the stories he told while he snapped away. He knew exactly what was at stake in those peace talks. What the Swedes were determined to keep, what the French wanted to get their hands on, and how even back then the Bavarians and the Saxons thought they could outfox the rest. Also that the focus of the war had shifted from religion to grabbing and holding territory. Which was why the small island where Camilla was born, and also Greifswald, where she later went to school and learned to play the organ, passed into Swedish hands for a long time. When people ask her where she's from, Camilla still tells them sometimes, From Swedish Lower Pomerania.

That same period gave birth to the song Taddel's father always sang when you spent the summer with us, Lena, on the island of Møn and couldn't get to sleep at night. Actually it wasn't a lullaby. It began with *Fly, May bug, fly,* and ended with *Pomerania's all burned down.* In the middle was something really grisly: *Pray, little one, pray, the Swedes will be here next day* ...

And it went on, *They'll pull out your legs and arms and all, set fire to your house and stall.*

Come on, Lena, sing it for us! I know you love to sing.

Only if the rest of you sing along ...

One, two, three: *Fly, May bug, fly, your father's gone to war* ...

But then all those photos your father took with Paulchen's help—of the parking lot and later the town, where there was a pilgrimage chapel with a Madonna who could cure certain illnesses—were developed in Mariechen's darkroom, and she used a trick that none of us . . .

No one ever got to see them, not even Camilla.

Your father merely commented, They turned out quite well; some of them were blurry.

But according to him, the Brückenhof came out nice and sharp. You could see how many outbuildings it had and that the hostel and the barns with their thatched roofs showed no signs of war damage.

He actually boasted of his skill as a photographer: Believe me, children! In one of the shots by the entrance to the hostel you can make out a person standing, a little fuzzy but recognizable. I'm sure it's the Brückenhof's innkeeper, a certain Libuschka, known far and wide as Courage.

And then he hinted at portrait photos he'd allegedly captured at the mill and in the Telgte chapel: On the bank of the Ems I got shots of a certain Greflinger and someone called Stoffel, who later became famous, and in the Chapel of Grace I have a young poet called Scheffler, kneeling and crossing himself.

But he didn't say any of that till we got to the Danish island where we spent summers, where Camilla was happy because your father was always in a good mood and the weather was usually lovely.

The old man never went farther with us than across the meadow to the beach; he wanted to get back to his Olivetti . . .

... and typing kept him in a good mood.

Whenever we went to Møn for the holidays, little Lena joined us. You were so sweet ...

... but sometimes you got on my nerves with your theatrics.

Well, that's how I was. As they say, practice makes perfect. If little Nana had been there, though, I'm sure I'd have been much less theatrical. But at the time I didn't know she existed.

Too bad you didn't come along, Taddel ...

... and all because the governor's house, which Camilla rented, so called only because it was actually a cowherd's cottage with no running water and no electricity, had only kerosene lamps and candles.

We didn't mind ...

... and in the evening it was really cosy.

But not good enough for Taddel; he wanted his creature comforts.

It's like the Soviet Occupation Zone, you said.

I, on the other hand, loved being on that island, even though I often cried because I missed Mieke and Rieke, my big sisters. In the beginning, when I was little, my papa would pick me up in Berlin. Later, after I started school, I took the train all by myself through East Germany to Warnemünde, then the ferry across the Baltic and the Danish railway to Vordingborg, where my papa and Camilla picked me up. I could have brought little Nana with me if my little sister hadn't been kept the family secret. No, no question of that. You boys treated me extremely well, even if I sometimes totally got on your nerves, according to

Paulchen. Before going to sleep, Jasper and I would tell each other jokes. I loved jokes from the time I was small. Oh, yes. We took lots of walks, across the pasture to the beach, where I made my papa happy by singing a song in Low German that I'd learned in school: *Kum tau mi, kum tau mi, ick bün so alleen* . . . Or we went through the woods that started right behind the house and seemed like a real jungle to me. I was scared, and kept tripping over tree roots and falling down, which made me cry. Can we do without the drama? Jasper would shout . . .

Even then you could recite whole poems by heart, which none of the rest of us could do . . .

It was on the island, in that cowherd's cottage, which to me was like a fairy-tale house, that I got to know old Mariechen better. Up to that time I'd seen her only now and then, when my papa was allowed to pick me up twice a week from my mama's. In his studio I had to play with buttons that he'd borrowed from Pat; as you know, he was anything but a normal play-father.

That's not quite true, Lena. It was me, your beloved brother Taddel, who got those buttons for you.

Does it matter? At any rate, while I was playing with the buttons, old Mariechen, who struck me as rather mysterious, photographed me several times with her equally mysterious box, whispering, Make a wish, little mouse, make a wish. Unfortunately I no longer remember what I wished for. Maybe—no, certainly—it was that my father would spend more time . . . Oh, well. But when she visited us for several days on the island, she had that mysterious box with her—Jasper and Paulchen told me all sorts of miraculous

and terrifying things about it. You remember, Jasper, the
time we all walked with Mariechen across the heath to the
rampart, as my papa called that long encircling wall?

Exactly. And the old man dished up the story he always
kept in reserve for when he took his and Camilla's guests to
the rampart. Supposedly he'd heard this story from Bagge,
the teacher who rented us the house. He always began with
a history lecture, because in eighteen-hundred-something,
when Napoleon ruled over most of Europe and the English
had bombarded Copenhagen with rockets and set it ablaze,
an English corvette—or was it a frigate?—turned up by our
island, in the channel that led through the sound to Stege,
possibly intending to fire rockets into that town as well. But
the peasants of Møn quickly drummed together a militia,
about fifty men with a captain at their head, who was actually a nobleman and landowner. The men went to work with
their shovels and in one night constructed an earth berm,
and in the middle of the enclosure they made a mound,
where they set up the only cannon they had on the island.
Yes indeed, they're supposed to have accomplished all that
in one night. And the next morning they fired that cannon whenever the wind favoured the corvette, and it tried
to set a course along the channel towards Stege. Naturally
the corvette—or was it a frigate?—pounded away. Day
after day, for almost a week. But then, on a Saturday, the
Danish captain of the island militia sent out a rowboat flying a white flag, with three men on board, among them the
owner of a large farm in Udby. The boat approached the
frigate, and the farm owner negotiated for I don't know how
long with the English captain, because the following day,

which was a Sunday, his daughter was supposed to marry the son from another large farm in Keldby. He explained that for a day the Danish militia couldn't fire on the corvette because all the men were invited to the wedding. So he wanted first to propose a short-term truce to the English captain, and second to invite him and three of his officers to attend the wedding as guests of honour. The following Monday, the farmer said, the shelling could resume. After conferring briefly, the English found this proposal acceptable. And that's what's supposed to have happened. Right after the wedding, at which we can assume there was plenty of carousing and slobbering of cream pie, the cannon fire resumed. It continued until the English warship simply turned round and headed back towards Zeeland under full sail, either because it couldn't get through to Stege or because it was running out of munitions. The rampart still exists, as does the mound in the middle where the cannon stood, though in the meantime the moat's been overgrown with weeds and brush. But Lena, you didn't want to believe the story your papa told us, did you? You kept exclaiming, That can't be, you're lying again. Right, Paulchen?

How can you expect her to remember? She was much younger than us.

But I'm sure Lena remembers Frau Türk and her refreshment stand on the beach, where she bought little bags of liquorice drops and liquorice twists for her sisters, Mieke and Rieke.

No way. Or only vaguely. But I suppose it really was that way, because my papa often told crazy stories like that, especially to help us get to sleep after Camilla, who was always very good to me, had rubbed our backs. But I imagine you had the same reaction to the stuff he made up, Lara. And little Nana, too, when her papa visited her at her mama's, which was far too seldom for her taste, and sat by her bed before she went to sleep. Just a pack of lies. Though some of them were delightful to listen to, weren't they, Lara? But old Mariechen, who went to the rampart with us, used her box, which I found so mysterious, to take who knows how many photos of the rampart and the expanse of water beyond it, which at times was dark blue and at times gleaming silver. She bent forward and took the picture backwards, between her legs.

Three rolls of film for sure.

Father could never get enough pictures.

Later, when it was time for me to go back to school, she showed some of those little pictures to me, only to me. Taddel won't believe it, and Jasper probably won't either, but you could see that this time my papa hadn't made up the story. The picture showed a crowd of Møn peasants, certainly more than fifty, standing in comical uniforms behind the rampart and the cannon. You could even see the ship in the distance, with two masts and lots of sails and puffs of white smoke obscuring the ship's belly, because it kept pounding away, Jasper said. There were pictures of the wedding, of course, with all the guests dancing in a barn, and the English officers joining in, the captain dancing with the bride. It must have been hilarious. Laughing faces all around. Only the bridegroom looked serious, unable to laugh for some reason. Mariechen also showed me a portrait photo of the captain of the Danish militia. In spite of his enormous tricorn hat, he bore a striking resemblance to Bagge, the teacher from whom my papa was supposed to have heard this story about the rampart, which was apparently true. Since then I've almost always managed to believe my father's stories, even when I had to say to myself, Typical, there he goes, lying again.

Just as we, sitting here talking and talking, can't be sure what he's going to talk us into next—and what will come of it in the end.

It could turn out quite embarrassing.

But it might also be amusing.

Or make us sad.

Even if it's only stories from long ago, when we were children and had all sorts of wishes.

Make a wish! Make a wish! But Mariechen's box did more than fulfil wishes. When she was furious on your account, or the wind was blowing from the wrong direction, or something else was gnawing at her—war's eternally regenerating beaver teeth—she would transport all of us back to the Stone Age for the space of two or three rolls of film—remember, Paulchen? Click, click, and already we were gone, slipping backwards in time, banished to the moors and fens . . .

You must have seen us in her darkroom, transformed into a small horde, the children, the mothers, and me crouching around a fire, wrapped in animal skins and chewing on roots, gnawing on bones. A shaggy assembly, with cudgels and stone axes always within reach, so that later, on the last roll of film, when there was no end to the hunger, you eyed your old father, just hanging around, useless, babbling his tales.

Or you saw that she transplanted all of you, but finally only Taddel and Jasper, both of whom refused to believe in her box, into the darkest Middle Ages, condemning you to child labour on a treadmill. Spoiled brats! she hissed, and snapped picture after picture of you, chained to the treadmill day in, day out, quivering under lashes. But even Paulchen does not want to speak of that, although she let him watch as she developed the pictures, a favour never granted to me, although otherwise she provided everything I wished for.

Snapshots

T HE YOUNGEST OF the eight children is about to
have her turn. Finally, Lena says to Nana, who has
hastily invited all the siblings to her rather small
room, located in a commune in Hamburg's St Pauli district.
After listening patiently, Nana will now have a chance to
speak. She has had to borrow some chairs, as well as plates
and glasses.

Since they have all come, it is somewhat cramped round
the table, where bowls of vegetarian fare have been set out:
chickpeas mashed with oil, a smooth mush of eggplant
seasoned with herbs, grape leaves stuffed with rice, endive
leaves for scooping up the mash and the mush, olives, and
Turkish pita bread. There is cloudy apple cider to drink. In
the midst of all that, next to cut flowers in water glasses, are

the technical sound devices the father has imposed on his son Jorsch.

It is drizzling outside, confirming everyone's complaints about the summer as either quite or totally rainy. Nana is still hedging, does not want to be the first to let it all hang out, as Lena suggests. She begins rather breathlessly, speaking so fast that Taddel—or is it Jorsch?—feels impelled to suggest that she slow down. She talks about successful childbirths, mentioning in passing the pervasive stress in the hospital, where there is a shortage of nursing staff, as everywhere. Tales from a midwife's daily routine, with only a casual allusion to a few short days off spent in Antwerp: Ah, we had such a lovely time there, the two of us.

Full of solicitude for her little sister—and before Pat and Jorsch can interrupt again or Jasper can start commenting on the vicissitudes of contemporary film-making—Lara, whom the rest all respect, comments, Actually you're doing splendidly. Your Flemish boyfriend is obviously good for you. You seem so much more relaxed. Let's hear your story now! Wonder of wonders, Nana clears her throat and begins.

As you know, theoretically I prefer to listen. I had no knowledge of all these things you'd experienced or been subjected to. Just as Lena had no idea I even existed till finally our papa couldn't keep his secret any longer and said, when she was already twelve or thirteen and I'd just turned seven or eight: By the way, you have a sweet little sister—or something of the sort. I must say, it was rather late in the day for him to come out with it. Anyway, I grew up as an only child, though I knew I had many siblings, and on the rare occasions when I got to see you, you were all very nice to me, honest. But then Pat and Jorsch were off doing their apprenticeships, and Lara as well, because you wanted to be a potter, which appealed to me because I also liked to work with my hands ... And Taddel, whom I hardly knew, had the pleasure of living out in the country, with Jasper and Paulchen, who weren't actually my siblings, though theoretically the two of you also belonged in the family — as my papa always said, there wasn't really any difference. I was the only one who didn't. For the most part I was alone, but I secretly wished we could be a proper family, cuddly, I mean, especially when my father came for a short visit and mostly talked with my mother about books and book production, but also about forgotten or banned books and such, till I spoke up: Hey, I'm still here! But often the three of us would go out together, which was nice, to get ice cream or to buy something for me, which I didn't want, because when I wished for something it was never clothes or toys, not even Barbies, but something else entirely, something you couldn't buy. When I started school, at first I found it interesting to have such old parents who had a lot to say to each other, rather than young parents like my classmates'. Yet theoretically the two of them always told each other the same stories, as if they'd been together for ever and ever. Usually about people who also wrote books, or had written books, or only wrote about other people's books. Once, I recall, all three of us drove into East Berlin, with my mother at the wheel, and she secretly picked up something from someone. It was something forbidden that was supposed to be a success when it was turned into a book in the West. That was pretty exciting, because right after we crossed into the East we noticed someone tailing us, and he was there on the way back, too. It's a spy, my papa said, who's paid by his firm to follow us. But often we simply went to harmless places like amusement parks, with all kinds of booths and rides, because my papa adores such places. So we went to the biggest fair, the Franco-German folk festival in Tegel, where I took ride after ride with my papa on the flying swings. That was heavenly! We could never get enough. Round and around, soaring through the air. You know, he always loved the flying swings, and I did, too. My mother was petrified and refused to go with us. You couldn't pay me to go on one of those, she said. And old Mariechen—whom I probably met for the first time when my papa brought her along to the folk festival, and who scared me a bit, just like you, Lena, because she always stood off to one side and watched—she didn't want to ride on the flying swings either. Not for a million! she said. But then she snapped picture after picture of my papa and me with that photo box of hers, which my big sister Lara told me various miraculous and spooky things about, right, Lara? She caught us flying through the air, round and round, and both of us feeling so happy. Sometimes he was behind me, sometimes above me or below me, but sometimes next to me, so we could hold hands. Now and then we twirled round each other, to the left, then to the right, and I wasn't afraid at all, because my papa was there and I had him all to myself. I was so happy! But the next time he came to visit and showed my mother and me the snapshots from the photo box, we were amazed. At first we didn't want to believe what we were seeing: in all the snapshots my mother was flying along with us on the swings, round and round through the air, just what I'd always secretly wished for: the three of us as a proper family. He behind me, she in front of me, and me in the middle, and then the other way around. It looked so nice and cuddly, because we were so close and could hold hands. But my mother, who'd been laughing in all the snapshots, and had also screeched a little in fear, suddenly turned very serious and practical. She called the whole thing an optical illusion and clever distortion of reality. But then she had to laugh after all: That's what comes of riding on the flying swings too much and never being satisfied. But even old Mariechen never breathed a word, I have no idea why, about my having a sister called Lena who was a few years older than me. And my mother dropped hints, but that was all. Later, much later, when old Mariechen wasn't there any more, and I was fourteen or fifteen, and Lena and I knew each other much better—and now we're real friends, aren't we?—my papa took me to the Tiergarten, where we spent an hour going round and round in a rowboat. He let me row, and he talked, if I remember correctly, about the persecution of the Huguenots, about St Bartholomew's Night, when so much blood was spilled, and all sorts of other terrible things. And then we went over to East Berlin, which was easy now that the Wall had fallen, and poked around Treptow Park, hunting for motifs, as he put it. What a fantastic time we had! You should have seen us: there was a sort of amusement park with booths and rides, and we took three rides in a row on the roller coaster, not only because my papa loved the roller coaster as much as the flying swings, but also because he needed this motif for a book. It was far from finished, but the main character would be an old man called Fonty who rode the roller coaster in the Tiergarten with his French granddaughter, and went rowing and such. And that's why we went to Treptow Park, where he bought tickets for three rides in a row. But that roller coaster turned out to be creaky with age. It was left over from GDR times. It groaned and squealed so much as it went round corners that we thought it would give up the ghost any minute. At that point old Mariechen was already dead, but theoretically she would have been there if she hadn't so inexplicably . . . Well, you know what I suspect. My papa said, Who knows what else our Mariechen would have seen with her box . . . He probably meant those things we most devoutly wish for, which sometimes come true, like that time on the flying swings when my mama, my papa, and I flew through the air.

That sounds very familiar. It wasn't only with you that the old man was determined to ride the roller coaster; it was with Paulchen, Lena, and me, too, during one of our summers on Møn, when all of us—though without Taddel—made our annual day trip to Copenhagen. We went to Tivoli, which was packed, and there were fantastic rides. But none of us wanted to go on the roller coaster.

He was the only one who did.

I suppose he was disappointed in us.

I'm telling you, he was bound and determined to ride that roller coaster, which was super-modern, with all kinds of loops and a really steep descent. It looked quite dangerous.

The Ferris wheel or some other ride that was more sedate would've been okay. Even the flying swings, which he managed to talk Camilla into taking, but none of us wanted to get on the roller coaster, not even Paulchen, who usually did everything to please him. And when I let him persuade me after all, he took all of us for one ride on that roller coaster. When I got off, I had to go into the bushes behind a booth and throw up. A good thing Mariechen wasn't there with her box. She'd certainly have had a field day with me puking.

Still, it's a shame we had to go to Tivoli without her. She always had to stay behind with our dog Paula—my dog, actually.

Back in the village, whenever a ship was launched from the shipyard, old Marie would be up on the dike, waiting in a standing or crouching position for the exact moment of the launch.

Usually Paula followed us. Mariechen had a habit of slipping her some egg yolk at breakfast, which annoyed Camilla no end.

I was allowed to carry the pouch with the rolls of film. You're my little assistant, Paulchen, she'd say.

Those boats built in our shipyard were coasters, small freighters intended to ply the coastal waters.

Every launch was a festive occasion. A big crowd would gather. Ordinary folks from Wewelsfleth, but also politicians and such. The mayor—Sachse was his name—stood on the platform, of course. Lots of speeches. Even when it rained. Usually a woman in a hat would smash a bottle of champagne against the bow. And the fife-and-drum corps from the town had plenty to do. But Mariechen never took any interest in that. She was completely fixated on the ship as it slowly, then faster and faster, slid into the Stör, creating a huge wave, but then came to rest quietly in the water just before it reached the other bank, which was overgrown with reeds. She stayed focused on the ship, standing with her camera at waist height or crouching, whether it was rainy or sunny, shooting two, maybe three rolls. Always focused on the ship. And I was allowed to help her change the film. Making snapshots, she called it. Afterwards she would go straight to her darkroom, right behind the dike.

That's why it was called the House Behind the Dike.

Father bought it after he finished the short book that followed the long one. That's what usually happened when a book sold well.

I don't know, really, we all don't know how he pulled that off: one best-seller after another, no matter what the niggling critics had to say.

Mariechen explained, Money matters to your father only because it keeps him from being dependent on anyone. For himself he hardly needs anything—tobacco, lentils, paper, a new pair of trousers now and then . . .

And when he bought the house behind the dike, he told me, Otherwise the shipyard will buy it, tear it down, and put up a concrete and sheet-metal storage building.

He'd heard that from the mayor, who was concerned about preserving the beauty of his village.

Father had to move fast to outbid the shipyard. It's worth saving, he said. Two hundred years old at least. It would be such a shame.

But his real reason for buying the house behind the dike was probably that the big house was getting too rowdy for him. Too much running up and down stairs. Our friends were always coming and going. I'm sure that explains why the old man moved his studio into the house behind the dike, with his standing desk, clay bin, modelling stands, and all his gear.

In the morning he'd go there to work, come back for afternoon coffee, then disappear again.

That was his routine when he had the caged rat as a pet.

He wanted to be alone with his rat.

Even Camilla seldom visited him there.

That's not true. The rat didn't come along till later, much later.

But he always needed time alone, everywhere, even when he lived in the clinker house.

Maybe he'd long wished for a rat he could be alone with.

Even so, I often went to the house behind the dike, because Mariechen had her darkroom back in the lean-to, and Camilla had furnished a cosy apartment for her in the old house. And sometimes, if I'd washed my hands, I'd be allowed to enter her holy of holies, as she called her darkroom. Every time it was so exciting. I got to see what she did there with the rolls of film she'd shot with her Agfa box from the top of the dike when yet another coaster was launched, and believe me, there was no trickery, no cheating. She used perfectly normal developer. And because Mariechen witnessed every launch, afterwards you could see where the coasters were heading, once they were fitted out and seaworthy: to Rotterdam or around Jutland, even in rough seas. And with one coaster—I don't recall its name—her Agfa knew in advance that it would capsize by the island of Gotland and sink. There were eight or more photos in which you could see the containers on deck begin to slip, until the ship started to list, and finally it capsized with all the remaining containers, after two of them had already slid overboard, capsized to starboard, remained afloat for a while, keel upwards, then suddenly went under, gone, leaving only a few pieces of clothing and oil drums floating on the surface . . . You don't believe me? It was true, though. The Wilster paper's headline read *Total Loss*. Camilla read the article out loud to us—the account of what I'd already seen in the darkroom in the stack of photos, the disaster the Agfa had foreseen at the launch. Later, two bodies washed ashore in Sweden . . . Dear God! Dear God! she exclaimed as the developing photos revealed what awaited that ship in the future. Don't you dare breathe a word about it in the village, she whispered, or they'll think I'm a witch. It's not that long ago that they burned folks like me. Kindling was always in plentiful supply. Always. Prayers did no good. It could happen in a flash. Then, after a pause, she remarked, Not much has changed since then.

That's what I always got to hear when she took historical snapshots, as she called them, for father: Hardly anything's changed since then, except the fashions.

And that's how it looked when she snapped a whole series for him in the main room of the Parish Overseer's Residence, when no one else was there, so you could see all the green and yellow tiles. And afterwards—right, Paulchen?—she hung up the prints in her kitchen, straight from the darkroom. In the middle of the big room was a long table, and around it sat a bunch of bearded old geezers, a good dozen of them, wearing these weird outfits.

All smoking long clay pipes.

And at the head of the table sat father, dressed as the parish overseer, in a puffy shirt and a wig with long, curly locks.

I'd be curious to know how she created virtual scenes like that without any of the equipment we have nowadays, because by itself that simple old box . . .

That's how she did it, Jasper, just with the Agfa. When Marie photographed the series of gravestones with baroque carvings in front of the church, the pictures showed Taddel's father as the pastor, in a huge white ruff and a black robe, following a coffin. Remember? The three of us with Camilla, looking for all the world like a grieving widow, trotting along behind him . . .

We had on black knee breeches, and our hairdos would have made you die laughing.

That scene seemed more like a costume drama than uncanny.

But you could only guess who was in that coffin.

Even the box didn't know that.

Maybe his rat, who bit the dust once he'd finished the rat book.

He kept that rat for a long time in old Marie's refrigerator.

Lay in the freezer, stiff as a board. No doubt he planned to thaw her out some day so the box . . .

Now you two are lying the way only my papa usually does.

But that's how it was.

I could tell you a whole bunch of things, totally crazy things, because I was almost always there when she developed her snapshots. Some of them were hilarious. She even made the shipyard historic, because just as our house in the village was still known as the Junge House, the shipyard was once named after Junge, too. He was the owner. Not till much later was it renamed the Peter Shipyard. Any number of whaling cutters were launched from the Junge Shipyard. They sailed with their crews, who came from our village, all the way up to Greenland and back. And it was such a cutter, returning from a long voyage and sailing up the Stör at high tide, that Marie had in her viewfinder from the dike, don't ask me how. And in the prints she produced, you, Taddel, could unmistakably be seen on board. I've wanted to tell you this for a long time. You were a cabin boy, wearing a cap with a bobble. Man, you must have been scared on the high seas, especially when it was stormy and the waves were rough. You looked completely done in. Like a dishrag. Pitiful. The captain on the cutter was your father, of course. Who else!

So? That doesn't surprise me. When I was little I was convinced he had a harpoon, because when he went off campaigning I thought he was going whale hunting, and when he . . .

It's weird that in another series of historical photos your father appears as someone else—the shipbuilder Junge.

Well, that's not so strange, because he shows up in all his own books, sometimes as the main character, sometimes in a minor role, in one costume or another, as if the book was always about him.

Yes, in one photo that Marie enlarged, though otherwise she never did that, you could see him seated as Master Junge in the big tiled room in the Parish Overseer's Residence. On the table in front of him stood a model of his famous whaling cutter. It looked like one of the models in the maritime museum in Altona. He had a long black beard and a tasselled cap on his head.

And his pipe, no doubt.

Maybe so. But we three were clustered around him, this time as apprentices from the shipyard. And behind us you could make out all the wall tiles, which supposedly came from Holland.

Right, from Delft, blue and white, which you couldn't tell in the black-and-white photos. At the time, Paulchen, you wouldn't have known that in the olden days the cutter captains received their pay in Delft tiles. And they in turn paid for their new cutters in part with tiles. They served as a sort of currency. I read that in a book on whaling. And I assume that's how all those tiles ended up in our house.

They're still there on the walls.

Some have windmills and girls herding geese.

There are also some that portray stories from the Bible.

Camilla explained them to us, remember, because she knew all the Bible stories.

And old Marie had to shoot every single biblical tile for my father, so he wouldn't run out of material.

One of the tiles had the Wedding at Cana. Another had Jacob wrestling with the angel. And other stories, too: Cain and Abel, and the burning bush. And of course the Flood, because the old man urgently needed horror stories like that for his rat book, in which . . .

It's amazing, brother, what the three of them experienced in the village while I was off on my farm with nothing but cows for company morning and night . . .

Or me in Cologne in vocational school . . .

Well, for me what went on in that godforsaken place wasn't okay at all; I found it dreary.

But apparently Taddel and Paulchen adapted very well to village life. At least that was my impression the few times I visited when my master gave me the weekend off.

We went to village festivals.

Wilster had a church fair.

And a disco, where I later . . .

You should have been there, Nana, because among the rides were old-fashioned flying swings.

Right, why didn't you come to visit?

Because . . .

You could have taken ten rides with your papa . . .

Because I . . .

And Mariechen would certainly have snapped the two of you with her box . . .

It wasn't possible, because . . .

You could have held hands . . .

Well, because Camilla . . .

Or your papa . . .

Stop it! Enough!

But I was happy living with my mother, though at times I secretly wished for something impossible. I like to hear all of you describe the miracles Mariechen, or old Marie, as Taddel calls her, could work with her photo box: those snapshots in which things from the past came back to life.

How about that, big brother? She was doing that when we two were small. When Taddel was a baby, and long before Lara got Joggi.

You weren't even dreamed of yet, Lena and Nana.

No god-awful mess, or who did what with whom first.

Old Marie photographed our clinker house inside and out with her Agfa Special so father could see who'd lived there before and painted under the eaves, where he now had his studio. It was someone who became famous later, and for a particular picture. He was a marine painter, did so-called seascapes. Three-masters under full sail, but also ocean steamships. Later, mostly battleships, armoured cruisers and such, when the First World War got under way and our fleet and the British navy were sinking each other's vessels in the North Sea. He painted the Dogger Bank and the Battle of the Skagerrak Strait, in which lots of people perished. He did one painting of a naval battle off the Falklands. Those islands are far away, down by Argentina. You could see the wreckage of a German cruiser, the *Leipzig*. In the background English vessels were in flames. And in the foreground a sailor was teetering amid the swells on a piece of a keel or a plank from the cruiser. With one hand or both he was holding up a flag. It looked like the flags the right-wing baldies wave when they want to get on TV. The title was *The Last Man*.

And this very painting Mariechen's Agfa Special re-
called . . .

Sure. Because her box was hindsighted.

I remember her snapping a picture through father's big
window while looking over her shoulder.

She contorted herself that way sometimes when she stood
on the dike, with the box facing forward while she looked
back, as if the past were there and in front only air. Totally
weird.

At any rate, the prints she gave our father later showed
that painting on the easel, still unfinished. In front of it
stood the painter, holding his palette and brushes. Behind
him you could see the big window in father's studio. And
believe it or not, next to him, in a uniform with lots of glit-
ter and a handlebar moustache . . .

And when we asked Marie, Who in the world is that? she
said, That's old Wilhelm, the Kaiser back then.

When I checked with father, he said, What Marie's telling you is true. The Kaiser used to visit this house. You can
read all about it in the Friedenau chronicle. Up in the attic
Wilhelm II visited the marine painter Hans Bohrdt. And
out in front of the house a single policeman in a spiked hel-
met stood guard.

She brought that policeman back to life with her special
lens. You could see him snap to attention when His Majesty
deigned to leave our house.

Much later—during the next world war, that is—when
the painter's other studio out in Dahlem burned down, he's
supposed to have become very depressed. He died soon after,
poor and forgotten, in an old-age home.

But the old Kaiser's supposed to have given the painter advice: You should put a crown of foam over here, on this wave, or something like that. So the painter—what was his name again? right—made some changes to improve his painting. You could see the difference when you compared them.

That's the kind of detail the box could remember.

Maybe what made the box special was not only that it fulfilled wishes but also that it could save the past like a computer, before any such thing as hard drives or diskettes.

That's why I pestered Marie: What's the special device inside that box? But I couldn't get a word out of her. I don't want to know, Pat, she said. It's a mystery, that's all! The main thing is, my box can see what was, and what will be.

That Agfa Special knew exactly what would happen later to our house. In the next war incendiary bombs would crash through the roof, dropped by the Brits or the Amis in vast numbers before they flattened everything with aerial mines and high-explosive bombs.

But the fires were put out quickly, so when our father bought the clinker house all you could see were a few charred spots on the floor in his studio.

Again the Agfa Special pulled off an accurate flashback.

That's right. You could see the bombs . . .

They were stick-type incendiary bombs.

. . . as I was saying, you could see them glowing, and someone—a different painter, who'd taken the place of the marine painter—tossing handfuls of sand from a bucket on the . . .

In all the smoke you couldn't make out the man with the

bucket. But when our father told the story for what must have been the hundredth time, he commented, You mustn't be surprised when the box shows things that happened in the past, Jorsch. It's survived far worse: a total loss when Marie's photography studio burned down. Not only her darkroom, but also all the stuff belonging to her and Hans.

And he always added, When Hans was at the front, he photographed with his Leica the events of the moment. First blitzkriegs and advances, later nothing but retreats.

That Leica still existed, as did the Hasselblad . . .

But they couldn't look back or ahead, not like the box. You saw it in action time and time again, and so did I: first with my guinea pig, then with Joggi. It even worked for Lena, when old Marie turned her into a comedy character onstage. Yet you liked performing in tragedies better, with tears, despair, and so forth.

It must have been terrible for Jasper and Paulchen when she snapped pictures of the ship that later, in stormy seas . . .

. . . as it was terrible for me when she showed me onstage as a comical old hag . . . No way! I had an entirely different vision of my career . . . For instance . . .

My mother and I saw into the future, just as you did with the ship that went down, but in our case the experience was lovely. The kind of thing one could really wish for, because even though we got to know Mariechen only towards the end, when my papa brought her along on one of his far too short visits, she showed us what her photo box could foresee. It wasn't just hindsighted, after all. So one time the four of us went for a walk on a beautiful sunny day along the Wall, which by that time was covered on our side with graffiti, odd symbols, and absurd figures. We walked to the place where you could see part of the Brandenburg Gate right on the other side of the Wall. But only after we passed that spot did your old Marie pose the three of us, my mother, my papa, and me in the middle—just what I'd always wished for—with the colourfully painted Wall behind us. She held the photo box far from her body and clicked and clicked. And my mother laughed and laughed. And then? A miracle! On my father's next short visit he showed us what the photo box had made possible: in all the snapshots—unbelievable!—the Wall was torn down. In each picture a bit more, till in the last snapshot you could see the three of us, with me in the middle, standing in front of a gap as wide as a door. The sides of the gap were all jagged, with bent iron rods sticking out. Through the gap and past the three of us you could see straight across the death strip behind the broken-down Wall and far into the East. Pretty amazing, isn't it? But Taddel refuses to believe it, and Jasper, too. We didn't want to either, no matter how happy we seemed in the snapshots. Theoretically the political situation hadn't reached that point. I can still hear my mother saying, Too good to be true. Unfortunately my papa took all the photos with him when he left. For my files, he maintained. I need them for when things reach that point. A few years later, the Wall was gone, and with it so much else, and old Marie with her box wasn't there any more either. My papa already had in his head the torn-down Wall and a story that ranged far afield, and he said to me, That's how it was, Nana, my child. Mariechen believed in her box because it knew what had been and what was to be, and what people wish for, such as the Wall torn down.

She must have been plastered when she snapped those pictures.

Things were going downhill with her by then.

When did she start drinking?

She'd always done it secretly.

Maybe she hid the bottles in her darkroom.

There's no truth to that, Camilla says.

I can hardly believe our old Marie was an alcoholic.

But she was.

And when Taddel got up his courage to ask, Well, Mariechen? One glass too many again? she'd reply, Not me! Not a drop. What are you thinking, you little brat?

The father sees the situation quite differently: she loved all of you, not just Paulchen. She could salve Taddel's pain with small-format snapshots. Lena shone in leading parts on stages large and small. In one photo series Pat, almost grown-up, could be seen smuggling parts of a dismantled copier into the East, which was strictly forbidden. Yes, in-deed, for flyers! She cared deeply about him, about all of you. She tried in vain to find the damn needle in Nana's leg, which was operated on several times, without success. And when Jorsch began to bite his nails . . .

But I shielded you. I forbade Mariechen to show you even one of the grisly photos she snapped—at my di-rection, to be sure—of the two sleeping cupboards, the so-called alcoves. Her box could go back to the seventeenth century and show the people who had slept in those stuffy cupboards—sometimes with legs drawn up, sometimes half sitting, some in little bonnets and nightcaps—slept there without waking, frozen to death: hunched-over old women, toothless greybeards, also peaked little children, carried off by consumption, or later the Spanish flu. No, I told Mariechen, these snapshots with all the corpses are suitable only for private use.

And not even Paulchen, who as her darkroom assistant knew more than he is willing to admit now, saw the alcove series in the developer tray. All those death-sleepers: parish overseers and their wives, the shipbuilder Junge, and finally his daughter Alma. Her store stocked liquorice laces and rock candy, which not only Lena, Mieke, and Rieke, but all the village children could buy for pennies . . .

But this is not enough, or else too much, for all of you. Yes, children, I know: being a father is only an assertion, one that constantly has to be corroborated. That is why, to make you believe me, I must lie.

Crooked Business

ONCE UPON A TIME there were eight children. Now they are grown-up once and for all: taxpayers, like Pat and Jorsch, they count their grey hairs; like Lara, they will be grandparents, if not right away; like Jasper, they will have problems with tight deadlines. All eight of them now sit together at Lena's. She has invited them between performances: We don't have much time if we want to have this thing in the can by mid-October.

And papa's supposed to direct it all? He simply dreams us up! exclaims Nana.

He puts words in my mouth I would never use, Taddel complains.

It looks as though some of the siblings might refuse to cooperate. Pat mentions a boycott, but then Jorsch says, Let the old man have his way, and Paulchen promises absolutely crazy darkroom tales.

Lena's rented apartment in Kreuzberg is on the fifth

floor of a renovated building from the turn of the previous century. Presumably this session will belong to Jasper,
Paulchen, and Taddel, but Lara and Pat have travelled far
to join them. Nana has taken a day off, because, as she says,
It's always a treat to hear the old stories that I would have
loved to have been part of. Jorsch has brought new con-
cerns. Equipped with technical details, he casts doubt on
the box again: The crazy part is that Marie didn't use the
more sophisticated Agfa Special to take all those pictures
but—I'm sure of this—the simplest model of all, the so-
called bargain box. They called it that because it cost only
four reichsmarks. It came on the market in '32, during the
Depression. But close to nine hundred thousand units were
sold.

He describes at some length Agfa's marketing strategy,
which called for potential buyers to save one-mark coins
stamped with the mint abbreviations A–G–F–A if they
wanted to get the box at the bargain price. People were lin-
ing up!

Then Taddel voices fundamental doubts: No matter what
she snapped those pictures with, afterwards she used all kinds
of tricks and dodges to draw us into her alternative reality.

Silence follows, which Pat finally breaks by asking Nana
why she changed schools a few years after the Wall came
down, And from West to East Berlin, of all things. And
then, to train as a midwife, you went even farther east, to
study among the Saxons in Dresden. One of the sons—is
it Taddel or Jasper?—cannot resist drawing the conclusion:
You became a real Ossie. And Nana replies, Theoretically
you could say that.

Lena has set the table with a generous platter of cheeses, olives, and walnuts, with plenty of bread. Paulchen is uncorking bottles of white wine. All eight of them, who from now on don't want to be grown-up, are eager to start.

So when was it that our father received the rat as a gift?

On his birthday, maybe?

Supposedly he'd been wanting one for a long time.

Worse than that. She was sitting in a cage under the Christmas tree.

And my papa said to me, Clearly the rats are going to outlive us, the human race—that's exactly how he expressed himself—if they can survive on the Bikini Atoll, contaminated with radiation . . .

Another of his sayings.

But it wasn't Marie who finally got him the rat, but Camilla.

And no sooner was the cage in his studio than Marie took her Agfa . . .

Hold on, Paulchen. The rat can wait, no matter how cool that creature was. Let Jasper tell us first how old Marie found him out when he was in trouble.

That's something I don't like to talk about. See, I had a hard time fitting in in the village. There was no one I could have a sensible conversation with, about books and films and such, I mean . . . That included the two of you. School wasn't so bad, but otherwise, what a drag. You boys had all kinds of friends, including some great pals. You even got a kick out of the village festivals.

And Taddel had a really nice girlfriend . . .

And girls from Glückstadt were always waiting for you, Paulchen, at the bus stop across from our house. Some were good-looking, too.

They cackled like hens and were crazy about you.

To which our Paulchen paid no attention at all.

You walked right by them, cool as you please.

Anyway, you were always out with your dog, heading over the dike. Paulchen and Paula walking along the Stör towards Uhrendorf, Beidenfleth . . .

He used to cut cattails and sell them for one pfennig apiece to the passengers at the ferry slip.

Or he hung out at the house behind the dike with Mariechen, who let him into her darkroom without a moment's hesitation.

Things got ugly when the old bag agreed to watch us, because father was scheduled to go on a long trip again, to China, Thailand, Indonesia, the Philippines, somewhere else, and on to Singapore . . .

He'd persuaded Camilla to go with him.

That must have been before he got the rat.

The two of them were gone for over a month.

Right, the rat didn't exist until much later; at most in my father's head as a cherished wish.

So much drama before they finally set out.

I remember the phone ringing and Frau Engel, our cleaning woman, shouting, A call from China! Goodness me, a direct call from China!

She raced through the house in a tizzy till she found Camilla: Come quick, please, come quick! Someone important's calling from China.

It was only the German ambassador, who happened to be a writer, too, and wanted my father to bring him some liverwurst, because you couldn't get proper liverwurst anywhere in China.

The village butcher, who was famous for the quality of his liverwurst, sealed up two rolls of smoked liverwurst for them, good long ones, too.

And they went along on the trip?

Packed among father's socks and shirts, maybe?

That's how it was. And later the butcher received a letter on fancy stationery from the embassy in Beijing, thanking him.

He framed it and hung it up in his shop, next to his master's diploma.

And shortly before our parents left on their trip, Mariechen snapped a couple of pictures of those liverwursts, because the old man . . .

Paulchen had to arrange them first one way, then another. Side by side, then forming a cross. She put the lens right up to them, crawled across the table . . .

And my father commented, I wonder what stories those liverwursts have to tell.

As she snapped those pictures, she muttered something incomprehensible. It sounded like Chinese.

But watching the three of us was too much for old Marie.

Once she threw her shoe at Taddel for being cheeky. You devil! You little devil! she shouted.

That's what she always called you when she got mad at you for coming home late.

She would flip out.

Took to drinking when no one was watching.

We didn't let on that we noticed when she'd had a few too many.

I was always up in my room, reading everything I could lay my hands on. Or was off in Glückstadt, where I had a friend who was into some shady stuff but was otherwise okay.

What was his name?

He was older than me. You don't need to know his name. He made an impression on me because he was absolutely fearless. No, Pat, I said you don't need to know his name. At any rate, there were repercussions, because my friend and I . . .

But first father and Camilla came back from their trip. They brought presents for everyone, I don't remember what.

But Mariechen didn't blab, that much you have to hand her, about all the things that had gone wrong, I mean. Especially with Taddel and me, stuff in school and such.

That's true, the old girl kept her mouth shut.

In that respect she was okay.

Not even pointed remarks about my girlfriend from the village, whose parents never went away and were perfectly normal. So different from my father. He came back from China with a crazy idea that had occurred to him there. He titled the new book *Headbirths*, and got to work on it right away. He based it on the notion that we Germans have no urge to have kids any more and are gradually dying out, while in China and elsewhere there are plenty of kids, actually far too many. It was supposed to be a short book.

At any rate, he didn't need Marie to help him with it.

He could picture the whole thing himself, so for a while she didn't have anything to do.

But maybe the photos of those liverwursts she'd developed for his trip to China provided enough material for his new book, because he used those sausages . . .

So Mariechen was unemployed. Spent her time running around on the dike. She had her Agfa round her neck and snapped a picture now and then, but mostly of clouds, or when the weather was nice she aimed it at the clear blue sky, where there was nothing to see.

And that continued, because when father finished that book, in which the photographed liverwursts played an important supporting role, he took a long break.

That we weren't used to, and neither was Camilla.

It seemed weird to have him hanging around the house behind the dike, just sculpting figures in clay.

He was brooding.

Maybe he sensed what lay ahead, I mean climate change or nuclear power or the future in general.

Well, the hiatus dragged on. It lasted a year or more, while for me everything connected with school became problematic again. I stayed back, and was sent to the vocational school in Wilster, where I . . .

But eventually you became a teacher, before you went into film-making, maybe because you . . .

. . . and Taddel wanted to prove to us . . .

You were well liked as a teacher, I hear, strict but fair.

For a while you wanted to join the police—that's what I heard on my farm. But I gather Camilla said, What will you do, Taddel, if we all run across the fields in a demonstration against that nuclear power plant they want to build right near here? I mean all your brothers: Jasper, Paulchen, and certainly Pat and Jorsch, too. Will you come along and beat us with your truncheon?

That I couldn't have done, absolutely not. Even though I had nothing against nuclear power . . . So I came up with the idea of going into the hospitality business. I even set out to try it.

What a scene that was when Taddel left for Munich.

At the railroad station in Glückstadt you would've thought everything was just fine with him. Marie made a point of coming along with her box, which she seldom did any more, and crouched down to snap a couple of pictures of you getting on the train.

And when the train pulled out she ran alongside, still snapping pictures . . .

And she called after you, You may be a little devil, Taddel, but I'm going to miss you!

Goodbye pictures.

We never got to see a single one.

Not even me. It must have been something terrible, an utter catastrophe in instalments, that her Agfa foresaw.

And sure enough, our Taddel had been gone for only a few days when the letters started to arrive, one every other day, all addressed to Camilla, none to his father.

They were all tear-stained, that was how homesick you were.

You poor thing.

The adjustment must have been rough.

Look, Nana's about to cry, just from hearing . . .

I want to come home, come home, you wailed, like E.T. in that film that came along later. The rubbery dwarf that kept wanting to use the phone, I mean.

The old man commented, It'll get better. This is something he has to get through. But then he agreed with what Camilla had already decided: Our Taddel has to come home. He's not just pretending to be homesick. He needs the family. And Marie, who often butted heads with you, also thought it was the right thing.

We celebrated when he got back.

That must have been so lovely.

But I felt pretty low when I came crawling home . . .

Don't be ridiculous. You were so happy to go back to school . . .

. . . though you got sick of it again before long.

Just like me. In that respect we had a lot in common.

Jasper was the only one who had no problems with school.

But you had other problems.

How come? What problems?

Let's hear the story about your pal in Glückstadt now.

Let's get to the rat first; that stupid business with me and my pal didn't come out till weeks after Christmas. Up to then everything was okay. Taddel was back, Paulchen was roaming around the village or hanging out with Marie. Camilla was busy getting presents together. She wanted to surprise the old man. And sure enough, under the Christmas tree stood something he'd been wishing for for ages, something we considered one of his crazy notions but merely smiled at, nice kids that we could be when we wanted to: a cage with a full-grown rat inside.

Where did Camilla find the rat?

Certainly not in an ordinary pet store, the kind where you can get hamsters, songbirds, goldfish, and guinea pigs like Lara's, maybe white mice with red eyes, but never . . .

She said she found a man in Giessen who raised snakes, and kept rats on the side to feed to the snakes.

Her only challenge was getting the rat to the village.

Well, the rat, which sat there peacefully in her cage, got the old man back on track with his writing. Put an end to his hanging around and brooding.

And that sent Mariechen off searching for motifs again with her Agfa.

But Paulchen, who was allowed into her darkroom, didn't breathe a word about any of it, except to say that in the photos old Marie snapped of the creature, more and more rats were running around.

Taddel's father had imposed a complete news blackout. But it's all right for me to talk now: all the prints—and there were stacks and stacks of them—showed entire tribes of rats, along with creatures like in horror movies, half rat half human . . .

. . . which the old man drew or scratched onto plates with a stylus: running, burrowing, standing on their hind legs, more and more, and then becoming half rat half human, all of which appeared in his book, which turned out to be a pretty long one again.

We weren't supposed to say a word.

It's a secret, Paulchen said.

More than rats turned up in that book. Marie photographed an unrigged flatbottom boat for him, which the village dockers had put up on blocks for repairs. It was in such bad shape it could easily have been scrapped.

But in the photos lying around the darkroom the boat looked perfectly okay, as Paulchen whispered to me, and it was plying the Baltic with four women on board, until finally, near Usedom, where there were lots of jellyfish, which could sing . . .

And one of the women on board bore a certain resemblance to Camilla, who was the captain, of course. Another one could easily be recognized as Taddel's mother. And—this I'm sure of, Nana and Lena—the third and fourth looked a lot like your mothers. One of them, I don't remember which, was responsible for the engines, the other for jellyfish research, because . . .

If I understand you correctly, it was a ship of women that old Marie's bargain box . . .

Let's see if I've got this right, Paulchen: the boat's crew was made up exclusively of women our father had been involved with at some point, or still was . . .

. . . and our mother right there with them.

That I can hardly believe: my mother on a boat, and with Camilla in command, too.

It was all there in papa's rat book. The story took a really bad turn at the end, when the four women put on their fanciest clothes and their jewels to seek refuge at the bottom of the sea in the legendary city of Vineta.

I had no clue. Not about the rat under the Christmas tree. Not about father's four women on a cutter or flatbottom

boat, whatever. I was far away. After I finished my apprenticeship on a Swiss farm, I went on to agricultural school in
Celle, and then landed on an organic farm in Lower Saxony,
where I was in charge of the milking and became politi-
cized in my own way. But of what was happening with you
in the village, with rats and such, I hadn't a clue. You didn't
say a word either, Jorsch, about cloned rats running around
as rat-men. Though after finishing your own apprenticeship you'd found your way back to the flatlands in the north
where our father, Camilla, and the three boys . . .

That was because once I'd learned all they could teach
me at West German Radio, they didn't offer me a job. They
were under a hiring freeze. Nothing to be done. I hung
around for a while. Then father offered to have me come
and stay with you in the country. That would be good for
your little brother, he wrote, Taddel needs you. And because
father had bought another house, this time the buildings
that had once been part of a farm out in the Krempe marshland, I thought, This is a chance to get to know a different
part of the country. So I moved to Elskop, which consisted
of one street on the other side of the Stör, and, just like my
twin, turned into a real country bumpkin. Out in front of
the farmhouse stood a huge red beech. And there were all
kinds of stables and barns. I lived there in a commune. The
woman in charge always knew what was what, or should be.
It was like a family for me, something I hadn't had in a long
time. And when I crossed the Stör on the ferry and came
to visit you, it wasn't just to see you, Taddel. I'd swing by
and check out the she-rat in her cage in father's studio. And
of course old Marie, who seemed small and wizened, as if

she'd shrunk somehow. I think she was glad to see me. My, but you've grown, Jorsch, she said. And then, because I had hair down to my shoulders, she snapped pictures of me with the rat. I'm ninety-nine per cent certain it was the bargain box for four reichsmarks from '32 that she . . . And the rat was brown, not your typical white lab rat. I could imagine how those pictures would turn out. We were used to such things, — right, big brother? — from when we were little. But she didn't tell any of us what was going on.

Nor me, either, when I came to visit. Right after my apprenticeship with the master on Dobersdorf Lake, who insisted that his apprentices not keep any secrets from him. He tried to make me read my diary out loud to him, in the morning at breakfast, no less, with everyone sitting around the table. I refused, but I didn't tell a soul, not even Camilla, and certainly not my father, why I left and went to Kappeln on the Schlei, where I found another master and finished up my apprenticeship under more normal conditions. Then I found work in a little dump of a town in Hessia, but it was too factory-like—mass production. So I went back to Berlin, in the course of which I fell in love with the student who helped me with the move. But I don't like to talk about that, how it turned out, I mean. My children can tell you later if they feel like it: how everything was quite happy at first in the marriage, but then went sour—no, Lena, I'm not going to talk about it—and how, much later, I remarried and my life improved. But I knew next to nothing about the rat and what my father intended to use her for, because he didn't breathe a word about it, even when he came to Friedenau and visited me. A couple were living in the clinker house with whom he put out a journal that was supposed to advocate socialism, the proper democratic kind. Then that couple had children. It must have been the influence of that old house—having children, I mean. And in the city I shared a studio with other potters, and sometimes I got together with my younger sisters . . .

Oh, it was so nice when Lara came to visit me. I was still a child, and I thought it was totally cool when you sold your beautiful pottery at the weekly market in Friedenau—much too cheaply, my mother said. But otherwise I knew almost nothing about the rest of you, about what went on out in the country. All I knew about the rat business was that my father had always secretly wished for a rat, and had mentioned to me . . . But I had no inkling about the ship full of women who had once been his, or still were, in the case of Camilla.

You weren't the only one, Nana; we were all clueless.

Because old Marie kept the whole thing a secret.

He always has something to hide.

That's why no one knows what goes on in his head.

That's complete rubbish. Doesn't he say, Anyone who really looks can find me, hidden in sentences both short and long . . .

It may be true that you can find something of him in every one of his books.

That's why they turn out so long . . .

. . . like the one about the rat.

I realized right away that it was going to be a long book, because Mariechen kept disappearing into the darkroom, and she let me come in once I'd washed my hands really well with soap. What I saw in there was crazy. Things you'd never see in reality: endless rat migrations, rat processions, a grisly rat crucifixion. In any case, no more humans, only rats, as Marie said when she pulled the prints out of the developer . . . I was shocked myself. But why would I have breathed a word to Taddel or Jasper? No one would have believed me when I told them what that Agfa could spit out. Jasper least of all. He only believed what he read in those potboilers of his. But when that crooked business, as he called the break-in, finally came to light, because Mariechen could prove with her box what had happened, he was totally shocked at first, but then . . .

Hey, hey! What's this about a crooked business?

Sounds exciting!

Okay, Jasper, let's hear!

Out with it!

We've heard more than enough about rats.

Okay, okay, I'll tell you. But Taddel and Paulchen already know the story. It involved cigarettes. I'd hidden more than thirty packs in a plastic bag under my bed. I thought they were safe there. But then Camilla, who always finds everything, was vacuuming one day and bumped into the bag. That's when the drama began: Where did you get these? You don't even smoke. Tell me immediately where these came from. She took the plastic bag downstairs to the kitchen and threw it on the table so hard that a couple of packs popped out. And the interrogation began again: Where did these come from? Who gave them to you? How did you get them? At first I clammed up. Everyone was standing around the table—Camilla, Taddel, and Paulchen, and Jorsch was there, too, and—of course—Marie. Still, I kept my mouth shut. Didn't want to rat on my pal. He was the only friend I had at the time. He was okay, but, let me put it this way, entirely different in temperament from me. It made a huge impression on me to see how he operated, completely fearless. But the more I kept silent, the harder Camilla went at me. Then Marie, who was still standing around the table with the rest of you, suddenly aimed her stupid box at those packs of cigarettes, and from a weird angle, too, holding the camera behind her back, and shot a whole roll, giggling. And she'd hardly finished shooting when the old man showed up, and asked: What's going on here? Marie answered, That we shall soon see. Then she shot another roll, as if that were necessary, sometimes holding the camera at waist height, sometimes facing away, and sometimes stretched out flat on the table. She caught the packs that had slipped out of the bag from every angle. Then she said to you—Paulchen, remember?—and also to Camilla, as she winked at your father, I can't wait to see what's going to come to light.

We didn't get so much as a glimpse of those pictures. No one knew what old Marie's box supposedly revealed. And you just hemmed and hawed, Paulchen: It's plain as day what those two . . . And my father, who did see the photos, just laughed afterwards: Nice job. You two pulled that off like real pros. You knew what you were doing.

Well, eventually it came out that Jasper and his pal, whose name he refused to divulge, had broken into a cigarette machine at a petrol station in Glückstadt when it was closed for the night. I must say, it was sheer madness the way you two pulled that off. Actually it was your pal who did the whole thing, as the prints showed, while you just watched or served as a lookout. But no one happened by. So the two of you had plenty of time to clean out the vending machine . . . no, not the coins, just the cigarettes. There were five different brands, maybe seven. And you shared them fifty-fifty. It was all there in the pictures.

And after that?

You must have got a good thrashing, no?

But not from Camilla!

Let me say this: it could have been worse. I had to pay for all the cigarettes from my allowance. It took months, but that was basically okay. Camilla settled the whole thing in her own way, without naming names. But the old man, your father, just laughed: I'm sure our Jasper won't do that ever again. Let it go!

That's how he is, my father. What's past is over and done with. I recall when I was eleven or twelve and we were living in Friedenau. That was the period when old Marie kept moaning, Such a god-awful mess! and I couldn't understand why everything in my family was in chaos . . . Well, my friend Gottfried and I pinched a few things in the Karstadt department store in Steglitz — a comb, a pocket mirror, some other little item. Gottfried took some nail scissors in a case. But the store detective caught us and immediately called the cops. They drove us home with blue lights flashing and siren blaring. Gottfried got a thrashing from his father, who was strict but also very good-natured. I could predict this would happen, so I said to my father, who'd never hit any of us, Please, please, make it look as if you're spanking me, and do it right by the window, because the boys will be peeking over the fence to see what happens, and they'll all think I'm getting a good beating like Gottfried. That's exactly what he did, too, without any ifs, ands, or buts. He took me over to the window, laid me across his knee, and raised his arm . . . ten times or more. And because unlike normal families we didn't have curtains, the boys outside thought I was getting a real beating. I also yelled bloody murder, so my friend Gottfried, who heard the story from the others, was sure my father . . .

And what happened with the cigarettes?

I don't know. I left soon after that. I was fifteen, almost sixteen, when I went to America for a year as an exchange student, which was certainly okay for me, but not so much for Paulchen.

You want to bet old Marie puffed away Jasper's share of those cigarettes, little by little?

I can picture that: at breakfast, with her holder.

My pal, by the way, ended up working for the tax collector's office in Elmshorn or Pinneberg. That was much later, when I'd become a producer at Bavaria Film and had started a family. But in America, where my host family were Mormons . . .

At any rate, I stayed behind in the village with Taddel, and would have felt pretty lonely if I hadn't had our dog, Paula, who gave birth to another litter, eight pups, of which all but two were taken by the vet, unfortunately, and put to sleep, no doubt . . .

. . . among the Mormons in America.

And my father spent most of his time in the house behind the dike, determined to finish that book of his, the one with the rat and the four women in the boat and all.

Those last two pups were called Plisch and Plum . . .

See, the Mormons have the custom of . . .

That's why old Marie was completely underemployed. Probably started to drink again.

Eventually we gave Plisch and Plum away . . .

She would go over the dike towards Hollerwettern and back. If she took any pictures at all, they were only of clouds and dried cowpats. No matter what the weather—rain, snow, storm.

In school things went from bad to worse for Taddel and me.

Finally your Camilla put her foot down: Enough. We're going to pack up and move to Hamburg.

Well, because there were supposed to be better schools there for kids with learning disabilities . . .

You see, all the Mormons . . .

It was a huge adjustment for us, and for my dog, too.

Father would have preferred to move back to Berlin, if we had to live in a city—to the old clinker house. The rest of us overruled him, though. He had to give in, as a good democrat, he said, though it can't have been easy for him.

But for Nana and me it would have been so much nicer and maybe even positive if your family council had decided to move back to Friedenau . . .

. . . and be close to us, which I'd always secretly wished for but never got up my courage to demand, unfortunately.

No one asked us, however. No one ever said so, but we were illegitimate.

Beforehand, I mean before you all moved to Hamburg and Jasper went to spend his year with the Mormons, old Mariechen died . . .

. . . in the city . . .

Not true. That's not what happened at all. I know what I'm talking about, because I was there.

Oh, come on, Paulchen. You're just imagining it.

You dreamed it.

The end was completely normal, Camilla told us. She'd gone to Berlin to be with her, when . . .

Then I suppose you all know what killed her, right?

It was because you were moving away from the village, and she didn't want to be left alone in the house behind the dike, with the frozen rat in the fridge.

No, no, she died because she was so old and weak that in the end she was just skin and bones.

A Masurian handful, as my father said.

But from a distance, when she went over the dike alone she still looked like a girl.

Besides, she'd been wanting to join her Hans in heaven for a long time. Or in hell, for all I care, as I often heard her say.

It was kidney failure, Camilla said.

You all have screws loose . . .

Now the father calls Mariechen back one more time before seeking a suitable ending for her: she stands there with her box at the ready, prepared to take the last snapshots.

Actually he wanted to have her death recounted in his children's words, merely intervening cautiously now and then to impose his version, but because all his daughters and sons—and especially the twins—claim to have experienced Marie differently and seen her from close up, because Lara is worried that even more secrets could come to light, and because Nana, who had to wait on the sidelines too long and has wishes she would like to unload ex post facto, the daughters and the sons will chime in with alternative endings; as a father, after all, one is responsible only for cleaning up the leftovers.

Everything is supposed to have been more painful, sometimes more embarrassing, sometimes less. This much is certain: up to the end, Marie snapped pictures from every possible angle, even in mid-leap. And had she and her box not existed, the father would know less about his children, would have lost the thread too often, would not have found his love through the back door, open just a crack—please, don't slam it shut—and there would be no darkroom tales, including the most regressive one of all, up to now not spoken of, or only hinted at: that tale from the Stone Age, about twelve thousand years ago, when famine set in, and in eight little photos the sons and daughters came together in a horde and slew their father—presumably at his wish—with their flint axes and split him open lengthwise with wedges, removing his heart, his liver, his kidneys, his gallbladder, and his stomach, then his entrails, chopped him in pieces, and roasted the chunks slowly over glowing embers until they were cooked through and crisp, whereupon the last of the photos showed all of them looking well fed and contented.

From Heaven Above

P AULCHEN WAS THE LAST to invite his siblings, and they all came, punctually. Because he and his Brazilian wife, trained to design and sew flashy fashions, live in Madrid, which is too far away, he suggested they meet at a Portuguese restaurant near the harbour. Compared to other restaurants in Hamburg, it is very reasonable. He promised to reserve a table.

Now they are all gathered. The meal consists of fresh sardines, grilled, with salad and bread. Those who don't want *vinho verde* are drinking Sagres beer. They all admire Paulchen when he orders in what sounds like Portuguese. This early in the evening the place is not very busy. The walls are draped with fishing nets, in which dried starfish have arranged themselves decoratively. During the meal,

Nana has described a complicated birth in excruciating detail: Finally the baby came, without a caesarean! In response to a question from Lara, Lena bemoans the budget cuts in the theatre world: But somehow we keep going.

After coffee — *Oitos bicas, faz favor!* Paulchen calls to the waiter — Taddel, whose daughter was born only a few weeks before with Nana's competent assistance, mimics the funny utterances of his little boy, who, Jasper claims, looks exactly like Taddel. Now everyone is begging him to perform his Clueless Rudi number, like back in the village, but he insists he is not in the mood, until he gives in at last and is roundly applauded.

Now even Lara is willing to, on request, squeak like a guinea pig, just as in the old days. Nana laughs the longest and begs her to do it again. Only Paulchen remains solemn and collected, as if preparing for something that must come out but is not yet ready.

Fortunately all the others want to have their say, Pat first of all. While Jorsch is setting up the microphones, for the last time, as they all agree, his twin brother asks which of the siblings has found it most annoying to have a famous father. No one wants to admit to having been excessively damaged or victimized by their father's fame. Lara describes the incident in her childhood when she asked him for a dozen autographs: He gave them to me, shaking his head, on twelve pieces of paper, but then asked, Tell me, little one, why so many? And I told him, For twelve of yours I can get one of Heintje's.

She cannot recall whether her father was disappointed

or amused by the swap. But he tried to sing Heintje's tear-jerker, *Mammy dear, get me a pony*. And then he went back upstairs to his writing and his beloved Olivetti . . .

With this reference Lara has given her brother Pat his cue.

That's just how he is. Always was. I have to work through it, he said. All of us witnessed how later in life he had to work through the stuff he'd experienced when he was a boy in shorts. All that Nazi shit, up one side and down the other. Everything he knew about war, the things that ter-rified him, and why he survived. Then, when the whole country was in ruins, how he had to clear rubble, and the gnawing hunger . . . Whether up in the attic of the clinker house in Friedenau or in the Junge House and the house be-hind the dike in the village, and now in his converted barn in Behlendorf, everywhere, I tell you, he scribbled away or pounded his Olivetti, always at that writing stand, paced back and forth, smoked his tobacco, earlier in hand-rolled cigarettes, later in a pipe, muttered words and tapeworm-long sentences, made faces, just as I make faces, and when he had something in the works again never noticed when one of us, my brother or me or you, Lara, or in the village you boys and Taddel, peeked in. Much later, even Lena and Nana realized what working it through meant in his case: one book after another. In between, shorter things, if he wasn't off giving talks here and there. Or had to defend himself, because from the right or the far left . . . But when we went upstairs and asked him for something, he would

act as if he were listening, to every one of us. Even gave us
a proper answer. But you could sense that all he really heard
was what was ticking away inside him. He told me, and the
rest of you, too, no doubt, when you were little: We'll play
later, when I have time. Right now I have to work something through, something that can't wait.

That's why he hardly flinched when the newspaper jackals jumped him, again and again . . .

. . . almost every time he finished a book.

Or he acted as though it didn't get to him. All snows of
yesteryear, he said.

He remained famous in spite of everything, which was
sometimes annoying, when people on the street . . .

It could be embarrassing when teachers got snarky with
us and said things like, On this subject your father has a
very different opinion, as you should know.

When we were living in the village he was actually har-
assed a couple of times, and not only by drunks, but also
when he went shopping at Kröger's . . .

On the other hand, they seem to really like him abroad,
even in China.

And when the mob fell on him again, Mariechen exclaimed, Those filthy attack dogs. Let them bark. They
won't stop us.

And she and her box kept supplying him with material.

Right to the end.

She even snapped pictures of his cigarette butts, and later,
of his pipes and his ashtrays full of charred matches, which
she arranged in a criss-cross pattern. Such objects, Jorsch

and I heard her say, revealed far more of our father than he admits, or is willing or able to recognize.

She had him take out his dentures and lay them conspicuously on a plate, so she could . . .

She'd lie down on her stomach to get right up close to them with her Agfa Special or the bargain box . . .

One time in Brokdorf—before they plunked down the nuclear monstrosity there—I saw him running barefoot along the bank of the Elbe at low tide while she photographed his footsteps in the sand. One step after another. A crazy sight.

And when he peed Camilla's name into the sand—out of pure infatuation, I assume—that provided an occasion for snapshots, too.

Snap away, Mariechen!

Because she was very dependent on him, not only financially, but also . . .

. . . and because our father needed old Marie. Always did.

Even before Camilla.

Maybe even before our mother, when he was still on the prowl, so to speak.

That's what I was saying, brother. Mariechen might once have been his lover. But what difference does it make?

Until just before the end, she still looked winsome.

At any rate, he often commented, What would I do without Marie, which made us think, or me, anyway—Jorsch was less convinced—that maybe there was something between them. But our mother never noticed anything, or acted as though she didn't, and neither did Camilla.

Anyway, no one will ever know for sure what happened between the two of them.

All I'm saying is, there could have been something. When I asked him about it—around the time when I was milking twenty cows on my organic farm and making cheese that I sold direct from the farm or at the weekly market in Göttingen—all he said was, This particular variant of love, which exists alongside others and doesn't depend on sex, apparently turns out to be more durable.

And when he visited me in Cologne, maybe to check out what was going on with my apprenticeship, he said, Of all the women I've loved, or still love, Mariechen is the only one who doesn't demand even a smidgen of me, but gives everything.

Well, thank you very much. That was the pasha speaking again. As I was saying, Marie was extremely dependent on him. Unfortunately, I must add. He used her, even though he may not have had anything going with her, purely physically, I mean. She admitted to me, For your papa, Lena, I do everything. I'd snap a picture of the devil himself with my box, to show him that even the devil is just a person. The photos she took of me were perfectly ordinary publicity stills, by the way.

Well, my image of old Marie is entirely different: when Camilla and father went off on one of their trips, and she was supposed to look after Jasper, Paulchen, and me, she let me have it while we were waiting for the school bus: You're just as much of a devil as your father, you are! Always me, me, me! Other people can go jump in the lake for all you care.

Well, that wasn't the tone she took with me. When Joggi was still alive but had lost interest in Underground journeys because he was old and feeble and half-blind, Marie told me, Believe me, little Lara, your father promised my Hans on his deathbed that he'd take care of me, no matter what, even if stones rained from heaven.

What a confusing picture. I don't know what to think. Each of you tells such a different story. Unfortunately we didn't get to see Marie very often. There was that time at the amusement park, which was so lovely. And later, when she photographed us right in front of the Wall. But my mother, who thinks she knows our papa, always felt old Marie was a kind of mother substitute for him, because his own mother . . .

You're all barking up the wrong tree. When I was in the darkroom with her and watched her developing pictures and so on, she told me plainly, The old man gets what he wants from his snap-away-Marie. But the only one I love is my Hans, still, even if he was a bastard like all the rest!

Okay, okay! Keep up this childish speculation if you like . . . We have children of our own, a whole load. Lara alone has five. Let them be the ones to tell the rest of the story, after Mariechen's death. I mean the bottom line: what's turned out all right with us, what got screwed up.

No doubt she could have said, Oh dear, oh dear, oh dear, or What a god-awful mess.

And I say you're all talking total nonsense. You have no concept of what a real god-awful mess is like.

Jorsch's life, for instance, is perfectly normal, with his wife and the girls . . .

At least that's how it appears.

And the same goes for you, Taddel.

Wherever you look, strong women are running the show.

It's the same with Jasper. His Mexican makes sure every-thing stays on track.

Just like Camilla with the old man.

They have sixteen grandchildren now. Including Taddel's youngest. And if Lena ever takes a break from acting and has a little one, and if Paulchen and Nana also have kids, imagine our children getting together to put us on the car-pet some day, as Jasper's suggested.

No way. Spare us!

Why not? All of them interrupting each other, like us.

Except that our children don't have an old Marie to snap pictures with a photo box of their most secret wishes, or of what once was and what will be in the future; think, for in-stance, of our papa's wish that for his eightieth birthday we get together to record on tape, without sparing ourselves or him . . .

Remember when he was around seventy and we all went to Stockholm with him, the boys in tuxes and starched shirts and the girls in ankle-length velvet and silk dresses? He told us then that he'd like us to let loose with our memories, without trying to be considerate.

But none of us wanted to . . .

What I remember is dancing with him as the band in the royal palace played Dixieland jazz . . .

. . . but he also danced with Camilla . . .

. . . right, to a blues . . .

We were amazed that the two of them still . . .

Too bad Mariechen couldn't have been there.

Yes, with her wishing box.

Imagine the crazy snapshots she'd have produced, a danse macabre. All of us as skeletons, and Pat hopping along at the head of the procession.

I'd like to know what became of all the negatives and the thousands of prints from her Agfa. If I add up all the rolls of Isochrom she shot of us, first on Karlsbader Strasse, then in the clinker house . . .

There must have been well over a thousand.

Supposedly father doesn't have any. I asked him once, Wouldn't they make a terrific family album? For instance, all the photos of Joggi on the Underground . . .

. . . or the ones where we look like people from the Stone Age, all shaggy and gnawing on bones . . .

. . . or Taddel as a cabin boy on a whaling cutter in rough seas . . .

. . . or Jorsch with his flying-mobile high above the roofs of Friedenau . . .

But then you should also include the lovely snapshots of me on the flying swings between my papa and my mama.

Of course, Nana. Something representing what each of us wished for or dreaded.

But also the series Marie snapped in the Wewelsfleth church of that old painting of the apple-shoot. And when she developed the photos, the boy from whose head the farmer Henning Wulf had to shoot the apple, because some crazy count insisted, looked for all the world like Paulchen.

And Henning Wulf looked like father, and was holding a second arrow for his crossbow clenched between his lips . . .

. . . that was intended for Count So-and-so, if the first arrow . . .

I thought that was a northern version of the Wilhelm Tell story, wasn't it?

Bad guess, brother! Historically speaking, that happened a long time before the Swiss apple-shoot.

And what became of all the rat photos, and the series of our mothers sailing around the Baltic looking for Vineta and finally, wearing all their jewels and their prettiest clothes . . .

Father pooh-poohed my idea of a family album: Anything worth using I worked through, and as quickly as possible, because after a short while the prints started to fade and the negatives yielded less and less, till nothing was left — such a pity.

He bemoaned the loss: I wish I had some of those prints. For instance, the early snapshots with the mechanical scarecrows. Or the series with the dog, showing him fleeing from east to west at the end of the war, and running, running. That would be something for my files.

And when I kept pestering him, he said, Ask Paulchen. He was there with her in the darkroom to the end. Maybe Paulchen still has some usable material.

There, you see?

I was thinking the same thing.

And you can tell us whether what our father speculated is true — that Mariechen would sometimes pour a little glass of her pee-pee into the developer tray, because only that way . . .

Come on, Paulchen. Out with it.

And none of that mumbo-jumbo about professional secrets.

I don't know a thing. I don't have a thing. You're all barking up the wrong tree. And the business about her piss—you
don't really believe that. It only occurred to your father because witches in the Middle Ages . . . Total idiocy. We used
perfectly normal developer. Our Marie didn't need tricks or
dodges. But she destroyed any negatives from the past. It's
the devil's handiwork! she exclaimed, and then, one Sunday
when we were alone in the house behind the dike, she decided to toss everything, all the negatives, into a bucket and
set fire to it. One flame shot up and the whole batch melted.
That was exactly a day after it had been decided that we
were moving to Hamburg, so Taddel and I could . . .

Away from that dump at last.

We were better off in Hamburg, no question. The work
at school was manageable, at least for me, compared to
Wilster.

But Marie wasn't up to moving. She got sick, looked posi-
tively anorexic.

And then my papa donated the old Parish Overseer's
Residence to some cultural institution, so writers could work
there for a given period under the eaves or in the big room
with the green and yellow tiles. That meant everything connected with us would be gone. Old Marie couldn't adjust to
all the changes, and practically fled from the village, back
to the city, utterly alone in her much too big studio on the
Kudamm till she got sicker and sicker, and finally . . .

It was really bad, because her kidneys . . .

She had to be hospitalized.

Mariechen, of all people, who was never sick and described herself as a tough old bird . . .

But Camilla made sure she got a single room.

It was a Catholic hospital, with nuns as floor nurses, and apparently a crucifix on the wall above her bed.

I heard that old Marie threw the cross at one of the nuns . . .

. . . because she wanted to wash Mariechen's feet, which would actually have been okay for a nurse to do.

But supposedly the nun said, Now, now, we want to have clean feet when we go to meet our Lord, don't we?

And Marie flipped—completely lost control, tore the cross off the wall and almost decapitated the nun.

Typical Mariechen.

A crazy story, which she shared the next day with Camilla, hot off the press.

And old Marie's supposed to have said, What a pity. If I'd had my box with me, I would have caught the old bag bucknaked, as her Lord created her, in a few snapshots . . .

She died a few days later.

. . . with her feet still unwashed.

She's buried in the Grove Cemetery in Zehlendorf, next to her Hans, obviously.

It's so sad.

So how old was our Mariechen?

No one knew exactly, not even father.

She could get really angry when something rubbed her the wrong way or one of you provoked her, just like Taddel.

But Lena and I heard she had a peaceful death . . .

. . . and not in the ward but in her own bed . . .

They say even in death she looked like a girl.

Sadly not one of us was there when she died, the poor thing.

Not even our papa.

She was all alone . . .

No, no, no. That's not how it happened. It wasn't in the city or in the village, either. It happened on the dike, and in the middle of a storm . . .

All right, Paulchen, tell us . . .

I was there. I kept shouting, Let's turn back, Mariechen! But she rushed on, heading for Hollerwettern, towards the dike along the Elbe. The sky above the marsh was perfectly clear but the gale was force 10, if not 12. It was coming from the east rather than from the north-west, as it usually did. That's enough, Mariechen! I shouted. But she looked as if she was enjoying it. Running in a gale. She was leaning into the wind. So was I, no doubt. The dog had had enough, though. We made it to the spot where the Stör dike meets the Elbe dike. But Paula had already turned back. It was high tide. Hardly any ships on the river, also because it was Sunday. I mentioned that she'd burned up the negatives in a bucket beforehand . . .

Right, you said a flame shot up.

But now the wind on the dike was gusting harder. At the same time, we had a clear view over the landscape and down the Elbe as far as Brokdorf, where the construction cranes had gone up for that atomic shit, a done deal. Then it became impossible to see, because the gusts were coming thick and fast. Mariechen, I shouted, you're going to fly away on me! But she was already flying. Simply took off. It must have been a violent gust. And light as she was, it pulled her—no, she flew, climbed straight up over the dike, up and up, was only a thin line, then a dot, and finally she was gone, swallowed up by the sky . . . I'm telling you, it was blue, perfectly blue. Not a cloud. Swept clean and blue. And suddenly something fell. Fell right at my feet. Yes, straight down from the sky and landed at my feet. It was her box, complete with its strap. It lay there, well, as if descended from heaven. But nothing broken from the fall. It could have hit me as I stood there on the dike, gazing heavenwards, where our Mariechen had been just a line, then a dot, and was now gone . . .

Typical Paulchen.

A complete fabrication.

You cooked up the whole thing.

Or dreamed it.

But it's a lovely image, old Mariechen simply ascending to heaven . . .

And then her box falls down . . .

But one can certainly imagine her ascending in a storm . . .

Light as a feather.

Go on, Paulchen.

Don't let them distract you.

Yes, please, Paulchen. What happened next?

At first I was totally beside myself. I thought: You're losing your mind. You dreamed the whole thing. But then I looked down and saw not only her Agfa lying on the dike but also her shoes, with her socks in them. I forgot to mention that as she lifted off, and I shouted, Mariechen! she called out, But with clean feet! At any rate, I saw her going up with bare feet, getting smaller and smaller. That's how it was. What was I supposed to do? I bent down, picked up the shoes with the socks, and the Agfa box, hung it round my neck, and, with the wind at my back now, made my way to the village, not along the top of the dike but through the opening in the dike and then along the road, straight towards the church tower. And because I didn't know what to do—Taddel was probably off somewhere with his girlfriend, Jasper was far away in America among the Mormons, and Camilla was in Holstein, campaigning with the old man—I went to the house behind the dike and straight to the darkroom. I wanted to see what was on the roll of film she'd loaded in the camera before she set out, saying to me, I just want to go over the dike for a bit, get some fresh air. It's so magnificently stormy out. Want to come, Paulchen? Oh, well. Now I could see that the whole roll had been used. I developed it, as she'd taught me. At first I thought I'd really lost my mind or had done something wrong when I was developing the roll. Mariechen must have taken those shots barefoot from above, as she was flying. Eight snapshots, and all of them as sharp as could be. From way up high, then higher and higher, from a totally crazy vantage point.

So? Could you see the village? The shipyard?

The old Parish Overseer's Residence, the cemetery behind it?

What I saw was the future. Everything under water. The dikes, because they'd been overtopped, were no longer visible. Nothing left of the shipyard. All that was visible of the village was the very tip of the church spire. And of Brokdorf, only the top of a cooling tower. Otherwise nothing but water, with no ships anywhere, no nothing. Not even a raft with a few people clinging to it. You remember that series of photos Mariechen made of us, in which all eight of us—yes, Lena and Nana, you, too—are crouching on a raft, looking shaggy, and gnawing on huge bones and fish skeletons, because she'd transported us back to the Stone Age? That must have been a similar flood, which we survived with a bit of luck. But this time no one had escaped. Or all the people—you could only hope—had got away just in time, before the water rose and rose, and—as we'd experienced up to then only on TV—overtopped the dikes, so the entire marshland, including the Wilster Marsh and the Krempe Marsh, was flooded. It looked utterly desolate, those pictures Marie had snapped at the end. Standing there in her darkroom, I cried. I had to cry because now she was gone, ascended to heaven. Only the shoes remained, and her socks. Paula sniffed at them and then whimpered, because she'd turned back just before Hollerwettern and didn't grasp what had happened. But maybe I also had to cry because in those last snapshots our future looked so dismal: nothing but water, water everywhere. After that I tidied up the darkroom, because Mariechen always wanted things to be orderly. And I cut up the photos, even the negatives. She would certainly have done the same, muttering, All devil's handiwork. But I didn't tell anyone about the ascent and those last photos, not even Camilla, not a word. Actually I don't believe that it will turn out so badly . . .

. . . or even worse: no water, and everything dried up, turned to desert, nothing but desert.

Or none of it's true and Paulchen just dreamed it.

Just like the ascent.

But what you see in a dream can still come true . . .

You're catastrophe addicts, all of you.

. . . so if we survive at all, then only in Stone Age terms . . .

And where's the box now?

Come on, Paulchen, what's become of Mariechen's box?

And how about her shoes?

Who has the box?

You, maybe?

Taddel means, what happened to Mariechen's stuff after she died.

. . . or who inherited what, after—let's just assume it's true—a powerful gust such as our Paulchen claims to have experienced helped her lift off and fly away . . .

. . . to her Hans in heaven . . .

. . . or in hell.

That wouldn't have made a bit of difference to her. The main thing was to be with her Hans.

Camilla says: Whatever was left of Marie, of her estate, I mean, was seized by the tax people, because she refused to make a will.

So everything's gone: the Leica, the Hasselblad, whatever else she had?

But surely not the box.

Which in any case was just a piece of junk.

So tell us, Paulchen, whether you . . .

It's quite all right for you to have it, since you're a professional photographer, and certainly . . .

It really would be okay if you . . .

I'm not telling you. No one would believe me anyway.

You want to bet he's spirited the box away, maybe hidden it somewhere down in Brazil.

Is that true, Paulchen?

Maybe you wanted to use Mariechen's box to snap pictures of the last Indians remaining in the rain forest, and whatever trees are still standing.

All right, where is it?

Right, where is it, damn it.

Oh, stop it, all of you.

Paulchen must know why he never breathed a word.

Everyone has secrets.

I don't tell the rest of you everything, either.

No one tells everything.

Least of all our father.

Besides, there were no more darkroom revelations after Mariechen and her box were gone, and everything became very boring, completely normal.

So this is a good place to end.

Yes, this is the end.

For me in any case, because I have to leave now and get to the hospital. I have night shift, like yesterday. We had five births last night, all of them uncomplicated. Only one of the mothers was German-born. The other four came from all over. I want to take snapshots of the five babies, by the way. I'm going to try to do that after every birth from now on. With a box I picked up at a flea market recently. It wasn't that cheap, either, but it looks like old Marie's. It even says Agfa. The mothers will certainly be pleased to have pictures of their infants. It's good for the memories, but also useful professionally, and maybe it will help show what will become of the babies later, much later.

Come on, big brother, switch off the microphones, otherwise we'll go on and on . . .

. . . because our father always wants one more tale . . .

. . . because only he, never we . . .

But he has nothing more to say. All grown-up now, the children assume stern expressions. They point their fingers at him. The father is at a loss for words. Loudly and emphatically the daughters and sons exclaim, All fairy tales, fairy tales . . . True, he murmurs in reply, but it was your fairy tales I let you tell.

A quick exchange of glances. Partial sentences chewed and swallowed: assertions of love, but also reproaches, stored up over the years. Now the lives portrayed in snapshots are called into question. Now the children have reclaimed their real names. Now the father is shrinking, wants to vanish into thin air. Now the suspicion is voiced in whispers: he, and he alone, was Mariechen's heir, and has the box stashed away somewhere, like other things: for later, because something is still ticking inside him that has to be worked through, as long as he is still here . . .